Afterburner Sunsets

Ver 2.5.1

George Saoulidis

Published by Mythography Studios

Cover art view outside is Jupiter and Io, from NASA/JHU-APL/SwRI/GSFC.

CHAPTER ONE

The double sunset cast a faint, secondary shadow next to the long one.

Dimitra bit her lip and held the hot chocolate carefully. She spilled some on the little plate below the cup, cursing herself all the way.

"What do you do up here every evening?" she asked, bringing the man his beverage and setting it before him.

He looked up sideways, lost in his thoughts. It took him an extra second to realise he was being spoken to. He pointed at the empty chair across the small table. "My girlfriend and I, we're in an increasing-distance relationship," he said with a sigh.

Dimitra squinted at him, shaking her head. "That can't possibly be a thing."

"Oh, it is!" he chuckled, opening his eyes in an expression of surrender. "I'm down here, I'm Trip by the way, and Persephone is up there on the generation ship." He pointed at the second bright spot on the sky.

Dimitra followed his finger to the fire in the sky. "I'm Dimitra," she deadpanned, still looking up.

"I'm looking up at the sunset, or, more specifically, at the afterburner sunset." He waved in the general direction.

"What's that? I'm new in town," Dimitra chuckled, holding the tray against her belly.

Trip sat forward, putting his elbows on the table. "Lots of people come to this cafe around this time of day to watch it, this is the best spot in town. Just before the sunset, couples show up and watch the golden-red sky. It's the only time that the sky is dark enough and the afterburner bright enough to be seen among the stars. It's sort of like Venus, which is mistakenly called the brightest star in the night sky. The generation ship's afterburners are powerful enough, bright enough to be seen with the naked eye. For a few more years, that is..." he finished with his voice trailing off.

"Wow..." Dimitra said, her voice small. "So romantic. So you look up at her, and she looks back on Earth?"

"She's somewhere behind that burn, yes."

They stayed in silence for a while.

He turned up to look at her, then towards the bar. "Aren't there customers to service? Not that I mind chatting with you..." he quickly added.

Dimitra plopped her butt on the chain opposite his and smiled wide at him.

"I-I don't understand..." he stuttered, looking back and forth. The place was busy and no one would notice a girl pretending to wait tables, despite her not wearing a uniform or anything.

"I don't really work here," Dimitra said and threw the tray like a frisbee. It clattered on the floor and against a table's leg.

"Okay... Then what are you really doing?" He nodded, seeming to get it. "You're a reporter, aren't you? The one that's been nagging me for ages."

"What?" Dimitra squealed. "No. I'm not. I just saw you coming here, then sitting all alone and thought I'd introduce myself."

He squinted at her. "But you didn't introduce yourself. I did. And you brought me my hot chocolate, you didn't act like a patron."

"Yeah..." she sighed, propping her upper body on her arms, her hands on the seat and bobbing back and forth. "I kinda do these things, you know? Impulsive ones. I really don't know anybody in town, I really am new here. And I thought you were cute and I saw you tapping an order for one, so I said, why not chat you up?"

He smiled awkwardly. "Okay... Thanks, but I just said I'm in a relationship."

She breathed out slowly, sagging on the chair with her entire upper body. "I know..."

They said nothing for a while. She clicked her tongue in an annoying way and he sipped his hot chocolate.

"I'm gonna go," she said and stood up. He must have said something to her but she hurried away, never having felt so embarrassed before in her life.

CHAPTER TWO

"Oh, yeah, push it deeper," Persephone moaned, recorded the videoclip and then pressed send. She stopped rubbing herself and waited seven minutes for the message to get to Trip. Then another seven minutes for him to get back to her... Sigh.

Her funk was gone. She stood up, put her negligee back on and went to make some dinner. For Trip, it was nighttime, just after a romantic sunset. For her, there was no sunset. Sure, the ship rotated but it was far too quick to consider that a proper day's rotation. They saw the sun rise and set forty times a day, and to be honest, she never quite understood what Trip saw in the whole sunset deal. Persephone puffed her cheeks and her finger hovered over the food selector.

Papapah... What to eat? Bland yellow food or bland green food? The yellow one. She pressed it and the food printer started to make her a corn bread. It was chewable, along with some jam. But she didn't have the credits for a new jar, so she licked the jar clean, rubbing the bread along the inside all around, making sure she got every little bit of deliciousness.

Mmm.

Yup, a nice dinner.

Her terminal glinged. She shot up, tapped to see his message. He was jerking off, showing her his abs, she liked his abs, a lot, and he simply said, "Oh, yeah, baby, take it all," while he breathed heavily and masturbated. Persephone could see it all, she'd asked him to position the camera that way. She sighed, her mood was completely gone.

Still, this was what they had available in their relationship.

Persephone sat back down on her chair and opened her legs and her nightgown, showing off her wares for the camera. She touched herself, finding it completely dry, which was not a surprise for her. This was pointless, Trip couldn't last more than five minutes, tops. He'd probably be done with himself by now, already wiped the mess off.

She forced herself to act horny, putting her lips forward and rubbing her clit between her index and middle finger. There was something happening, something... Ah... yeah...

Nope.

She sent the clip like that, pretending to get off. She added a bit of text, "Baby, I came sooo hard! You were amazing, your dick is so perfect." Then she added some surprised and naughty emojis, and tapped 'send.'

Persephone sighed, then licked the edge of her lips, she had jam there. She licked her fingers, which tasted more like her pussy than strawberry jam, and then stood up, putting her pajamas on again. It was cold in space. The only good that came out of this whole deal was that her tits looked tight and pointy on camera for her boyfriend.

Feeling cold, sad, hungry, and unsatisfied, she crawled inside her tiny bunk before her younger sister returned.

Zoe walked in with her eyes covered. "Are you done sexting?" She felt her way around the tiny quarters, it wasn't that hard to memorise it all. "Eww, something is sticky over here."

"It's just jam," Persephone snapped at her. The little cunt was so annoying, sometimes she swore she wanted to choke her.

Zoe looked at her hand. "Oh, right. Phew, dodged a bullet there!" Then she turned to Persephone. "Wait, you didn't use this during..." She trailed off, nodding with innuendo.

"Jeez, no!" I just got hungry, had dinner.

"Oh. Saved some for me?"

"You know the answer to that is negatory."

"Fuck you too, sis." Zoe crawled into her own bunk bed, which required her to step on the side of Persephone's to get up there.

"Ow! My leg, watch it."

"Not my fault you're all over the place," Zoe said with no remorse and vanished under her own bedsheets.

There was a long silence.

"It's pointless," Persephone said softly.

"What is?"

"My relationship. Trip, all of this! It's not like we can ever hope to meet in person! Heck, we're literally flying kilometres apart every second that passes."

Zoe's head appeared from the side of the bunk bed, her short hair falling around her face. "It sucks, Persephone, I know. Do you love him?"

"Yes!" Persephone spat back. "Fuck, yes, I do love him! But it's hard, you know? And it's getting harder every day..."

Zoe frowned and pressed her lips in a worried expression. She reached down and held her hand there.

A second passed, and then Persephone reached out and held it.

"You know, sometimes you're not that much of a little cunt," she nodded.

"And sometimes, I can understand what you're going through, sis," Zoe said, putting her face back on the side of her matress, but still holding on.

A minute passed.

"Can I let go? I'm getting sore over here."

"Not yet," Persephone said. She pressed her eyes shut, taking it in. Then she let go. "Now you can let go."

Zoe's hand vanished back on the top bunk.

She heard a sniff. Then another. "What's that smell? Persephone, eww!"

CHAPTER THREE

Trip squinted at her. "You're here again," he said sharply, but he seemed a lot less annoyed than he pretended to be.

Dimitra plopped herself on the chair opposite the table. "Okay, hear me out. I'm not a stalker, by the way. It’s just… I’ve been thinking about your situation all day, and I have come up with a possible solution for you.”

Trip frowned, yet again. "Solution to what exactly?” He made a fist on the table, he seemed to want his chocolate right about now. The setting was the same as yesterday, the afterburner sunset, the quiet buzz of the café, the golden-red hues everywhere. He was a fine-looking man, he seemed to work out and had good taste in clothes.

Dimitra chuckled awkwardly, fumbling for the words. She leaned forward, resting her elbows on the table and making it jostle. Thankfully there were no cups on it, or she would have spilt something for sure. You clumsy idiot, you. "Heh. Okay, give me like five minutes, let me explain my idea to you and you promise me you'll think it over, okay?"

He shrugged, crossing his legs and turning to the side. His entire body language was evasive. "I have no idea what you want. And you're spoiling my romantic moment here, to be honest."

"Yes. I am. And I'm sorry, but that's what I wanted to talk to you about. Listen to me once and if you say 'no' I won't bother you again, alright?"

He shrugged again, waving her to get on with it and then crossed his arms over his chest.

"You're in an increasing-distance relationship, right?"

He nodded. Of course he did, she wasn't saying anything new so far.

"The problems with regular long-distance relationships have been dealt with with the proper tech, teledildonics, videocalls, sensory feedback, VR, the works."

Trip scrunched up his nose, shaking his head. "I-I don't really like those things. I mean, of course we tried them, but they were, I dunno… Too-Too much in the way, you know?"

"I get you, completely!" Dimitra said, excited. She forced herself not to squeak like a chicken, she did that when she got excited. She grabbed the salt and pepper from the table and demonstrated the ever-increasing distance between them. "The generation ship flies further and further, away from the solar system. And you're in love, you wanna hang out, you don't wanna break up, it hurts too much. I get it, I really do. And people in love wanna have sex, you know. It's only natural, no judgies there." She raised a finger in the air. "But! The distances keep increasing, the lag becomes a bother, it ruins all the fun." She leaned forward, her eyes wide. "What if we put an intermediary body?" She winked at him. "Huh?"

Trip uncrossed his arms and turned to her. "I'm not sure what you're suggesting."

Dimitra licked her lips and looked around. She stole a pepper shaker from the table next to them. The woman there protested, "Hey!"

"I'm doing for it love, you dolt," Dimitra said and placed the pepper shaker in the middle of the other two on their table. She shut her eyes, flailing her arms around as she explained. "Okay, now here's the kicker. You're the salt shaker, okay? And this is Persephone," Dimitra tapped the original pepper shaker.

"How do you know Persephone's name?" Trip frowned.

Dimitra winced. "It's on your social media profile. Come on, it's not like I'm stalking you, it's floating next to you in Augmented Reality. Big deal. Check your privacy settings if you don't want people knowing it."

Trip grunted for a while, but let it go. "Okay. I'm still waiting for this big idea of yours. Sunset is almost over."

Dimitra tapped the pepper shaker she stole and placed it between them. "What if, we link up Persephone and me, and sleep with you with her commands exactly? And I fill in the gaps when there's a communication lag, by getting to know what she wants from you etcetera etcetera," Dimitra blurted out and rolled her hands in front of her.

Trip blinked slowly. He leaned back on his chair and looked away. "Heh…"

Dimitra tapped the shakers, rapping on them like a drummer. "Well? Just tell me what you think. I can handle it, Trip. Really."

"You want me, to sleep with you, while you surrogate for my girlfriend? And she'll tell you how to act and what to do, you'll carry on during the gaps, and she'll tell you in the next interval etcetera."

Dimitra shook her head up and down furiously. "Pretty much, yeah."

Trip smiled. "And how much is this gonna cost me?"

"What?" It was her turn to blink.

"You're a prostitute, right?" he declared with his palm up. "I don't mind your profession, heck I've been a john a couple of times, but I don't like the way you're approaching me."

"No. No!" Dimitra stood up. "I'm not a hooker, Trip!" she shouted, grabbing the attention of everyone in the café.

Trip grabbed her by the arm and sat her down. "Can you be quiet, dammit?" he said through gritted teeth.

"Yes," Dimitra pouted like a scolded child. "Sorry about that. But I'm not a hooker," she said softly, bringing her fist down her knee.

"Okay, alright. But you have to admit it sounds fishy. I mean, I don't even know you, Dimitra," he said her name as if he didn't believe it was her real one.

"I get it," Dimitra assured him, "I really do. And we can get to know each other first, perhaps a date. Yeah, a date would be a great idea. And then I'd need to get to know Persephone, you know, see what she likes and so on. And if everyone is on board, we just go for it, you know?" she ended with a grunt, mimicking a slight thrusting motion with her waist. "Just like in any threesome. Eeeverybody needs to be cool with it." She made a smooth gesture with a swipe of her palm in the air.

Trip closed his eyes and touched the bridge of his nose. "This is insane, Dimitra! And I'm still not convinced that you don't want money out of this."

Dimitra showed her teeth, looking around the café. "I'm not a hooker. How many times I gotta tell you-"

"Alright!" he interrupted. "Then what do you get out of this?"

Dimitra snorted. "Besides getting laid? Well, I can do my thesis on it, with your permission, you and Persephone's too?"

Trip stared at her for a minute. Then he slapped his hands on the table and stood up. The waitress brought his chocolate. "I don't want it now, sorry. You can charge my paycard for it anyway," he said and left the café.

The waitress turned to Dimitra. "Do you want it? It's hot."

Dimitra wiped the side of her eye. "Yes," she sniffled quietly.

"It goes well with the afterburner sunset, after all."

CHAPTER FOUR

Persephone went to work. As a second-generation colonist, she was born on the ship and she knew the whole thing top to bottom. They used to run all over as kids, despite the grown ups' protests. Now that she was in her twenties, it was her turn to scold the little buggers that did the same.

"Get outta here, damn you!" she spat at the kids, waving her mop at them menacingly.

They stuck out their tongue and ran circles around her one last time before running off to bother someone else.

Persephone sighed, propped herself up on her mop. She would have to do the whole thing again. The job was pointless, if they wanted to, they could ask the drones to do these chores. But the colonists needed something to do, and apart from the very important jobs like mechanics and hydrofarmers the rest simply went on the jobs rota just to find something to occupy their minds. It was a special kind of hell, knowing that you were stuck inside a spaceship that literally, physically could not turn back right now after reaching this speed, and that you were only the first generation, a mere ancestor of those glorious future colonists that would reach the target planet.

Nothing mattered along the way. All they had to do was survive. Sure, space was dangerous, and sure, they could get a hull breach and get wiped out in a fraction of a second and this titanic endeavor would all go to waste, but people couldn't live with that kind of danger looming over them. They simply ignored it. It was like Trip said to her when she was terrified of him going out during a thunderstorm. 'Yes, baby,' he had said, 'I might get struck by lightning, the chances are small but they're there. However, I can't live my life in fear. So I'm gonna go out now, and I'll call you when I'm back.'

She waited those agonizing minutes while he got home from work in that thunderstorm. Persephone kept watching the Earth TV channels that reported on the damages and the weather.

Weather.

That thing scared her shitless.

There was no weather inside the generation ship. Everything was monitored, calm and slightly cold. There was a microclimate inside the hydrofarms, it had a breeze sometimes. Mostly it was humid and once, Persephone saw a tiny cloud forming in the middle of the rotation axis that had no gravity. That was funny.

But nothing like those thunderstorms!

When Trip finally got back, he replied to each one of her two hundred messages. He was so patient with her, whenever she went nuts like that, or when she couldn't understand the Earth's problems and situations. For example, Persephone couldn't possibly imagine a life of abundance. She had gotten him to recycle his old tablet, he wanted to just throw it away! On the ship, they threw nothing away, it all got recycled. And the 3D printers could fabricate anything, even the latest tech and dresses from Earth if you got someone to send them to you, but the materials were extremely limited.

Persephone mopped the floor and watched it as it dried. The kids didn't come again to step all over the corridor.

She was done for today. She checked her messages. Her sister sent her something silly she found on the net. Her mother wanted her to bring back tomato juice from the shop. Her cousin wanted to hang out. No messages from Trip.

CHAPTER FIVE

Dimitra went to the café the next evening, just in time to see the afterburner sunset. Trip wasn't there. She felt a pang of guilt, about ruining Trip's romantic night. Yes, he basically sat there all alone watching up at spaceship farts, but still.

It was romantic.

And tragic.

Two people in love who had never ever met in person, and who had no chance of ever doing so.

The more she pondered this situation the better it fit her thesis idea. It was brilliant, nobody had ever done such a thing, nobody. Analysing this kind of long-distance relationship? Attempting to bridge the gap?

Madness.

So it was right in her alley.

Dimitra swiped up and loaded Trip's social profile in her augmented reality. She could contact him directly, but she decided not to bother the man any more. Instead, she created an ARO, an augmented reality object that was tied to a specific location. It was like leaving a note, but on the veil. If Trip came back here, which Dimitra was sure he would eventually, and if he wanted to, he could open the message and read it. She put on a silly animated cat that said she was sorry, and typed out the message on the virtual keyboard, effectively tapping her fingers on the bare table.

When she was done, she stood up and left the café before the sunset was over.

CHAPTER SIX

"You want what?" Persephone screamed into the camera. Then she had to wait seven minutes for him to respond, but her anger didn't evaporate in the slightest.

She sent some more texts. It would come as a barrage of messages to Trip, but she didn't care. She needed to vent in real-time. "Are you breaking up with me, trying to let me down easy or what?"

She paced up and down, kicked a cupboard, shouted 'Ow!' and cursed at her throbbing toe, and then sent more texts.

"You got bored, didn't you?"

"Don't bother replying, you bastard."

"No, I changed my mind. I do want you to reply, I wanna see how you'll try to spin this, sleeping with another woman."

"Screw you!"

"No… sorry baby, I love you."

"I'll chop your dick off."

Trip replied to the messages, but his explanations did not make it any better. "No, baby, hear me out. It's for research, for increasing-distance relationships. It's never been done before. And we will only do it if you're comfortable with it, I swear. You can talk to Dimitra, she's annoying but kinda nice."

"Oh. Oh, she's nice now, is she?"

"Not like that… I meant that I'm sure you'll at least consider it if you talk to her. I can send you her social profile, it's your call."

"My call? Mine? I'm stuck in a spaceship, Trip! It's not like I can stop you from doing anything with your new slut."

"Persephone. It's not like that, I swear. Look, calm down, and we'll talk later, alright? I gotta go to work."

Persephone stared at her comms, wide eyed. Her sister came barging in, licking a spoon of honey. "What's up."

Persephone scoffed at the comms. "Ha! He just left the conversation." She sat on the bottom bunk and pulled her legs close to her body, hugging them tight. "He's gonna break up with me," she said in shock.

Zoe licked her honey, treasuring it. "Come on, Trip? Nah, the poor bastard is in love with you."

Persephone shook her head, grabbed the pillow and hugged it tight. She pouted. "Nonono. He said he wanted to have sex with some Dimitra he met at our café."

Zoe shrugged. "So, let him." She licked her spoon.

"What?" Persephone snapped back at her, throwing her the pillow.

Zoe expertly dodged it, straightened her back and kept on

licking. "It's not like you can do it with him. So why not? The man probably has the bluest balls on the planet."

Persephone grunted loudly. "Argh! Why do I even listen to you? You're a teenager. Go frolic around somewhere." She shooed her sister away.

"I don't have any friends, not really. Plus, your drama is always the best entertainment."

At that moment Persephone shouted some incoherent battle cry, grabbed her sister and pushed her down on the bed, pinching her thigh.

"Ow! Lemme go," Zoe complained, thrashing around.

"You mean little… psycho."

"Lemme go! I'll give you some honey."

"I don't want your honey." Persephone pinched her sister some more until her skin reddened, but even she knew that her anger was misdirected.

She pushed her away and Zoe fell on the floor. "Ow, bitch…" her sister whined and held her head. She stood up, ready to cry.

"Oh…" Persephone stood up and hugged her, kissing her sister's head bump. "I'm sorry… I'm so sorry."

"Okay," Zoe said, pressing her lower lip. "But no honey for you."

Persephone waited a while in the hug and then pushed her sister away. Zoe reached down and picked up her spoon. It was dirty. "Aww, what a waste. That still had a good two licks left."

Dimitra felt anxious. She had taken a shower, dolled herself up. Heck, she had even put on her good bra, the one that didn't fit like a glove over her boobies. She was aware of it every time she moved but nope, she wouldn't complain.

This was what she asked for, and Trip was open to discussing it. That was all she ever wanted.

So, why was she feeling like a teenager going to her first date?

The self-driving taxi was there waiting for her, always on time, like the ad jingle said. She opened the door, frowned, and slammed it shut again.

She ran back home and took a pee. God, she felt nervous. She got outside once again, got in the taxi and spoke the café's address.

The taxi whirred and took her to her sunset date.

CHAPTER SEVEN

This time, Trip smiled when he saw her from afar. That was a nice for a change. So she told him, right off the bat. "Hey, Trip. How great is it to see your polite side for a change, am I right?" She bobbed her head up and down, her palms up.

Trip winced. He stood up and pulled a chair for her. "Yes, I'm sorry for how I behaved earlier. It's just that-"

Kate sat down, clutching her bag. "Dude," she interrupted him, "I get it. I showed up out of the blue, being my usual crazy self. It's fine." She waved the whole thing away.

Trip sat down opposite her. "That's good. So, let's do this again, shall we? I'm Trip, nice to meet you," he offered his hand.

Dimitra snorted but shook it. "I'm Dimitra, nice to meet you too."

"And you had an idea in mind, Dimitra," he said, stating the words clearly.

Dimitra found that odd. She whispered, mimicking the words, "Is she connected?"

"Of course Persephone is connected, Dimitra," he replied clearly. "I wouldn't go on a date without my girlfriend's approval."

Dimitra squinted, mulling it over. "Wait, let me get the logistics here. She gets a constant streaming from you, live but with a seven-minute lag. So I can ask her anything and Persephone can reply to this after seven minutes." She fanned her face with her hand. "Whoo. Now I'm feeling hot. Are you feeling hot? I shouldn't get a hot chocolate, not like last time."

Trip glared at her.

"L-Like the last time I ambushed you, it was totally not a date. Not a date, no siree." She popped her lips a few times, looking over the menu that appeared in her veil. "Yeah, I'm gonna order a strawberry soda. Thanks."

The table glinged and her order was underway.

Dimitra tapped the table. "So…"

"So." Trip smiled awkwardly. He mulled it over as well, and he finally broke the silence. "Well, we have some time, tell us your idea. Persephone is listening. I'm sure you can explain it better than me, it is after all your thesis."

Dimitra blinked. "Wow, this is like presenting it to the board. Right." She licked her lips. "I stumbled on Trip here completely by accident. I just saw him here all alone, and yes, I'm new to the city, I don't know anyone. I thought about, you know, chatting him up. Making a friend, or at least, spend a couple of minutes with someone. And he told me about your situation, the increasing-distance relationship. Basically, he shooed me off, but as soon as I went home, it got me thinking: Nobody has ever studied this particular kind of relationship before! Everything else has been done to death, gay, trans, poly, but increasing-distance? Never, I checked. And I came up with both a solution to your intimacy problem and a kickass idea for my thesis! Wow, right?"

Trip waited a second, then responded, pointing down with his finger. "Yeah, the disconnect takes some time to get used to. We call it discommunication."

Dimitra snorted, then reeled herself in. You're trying to make a good impression, stupid. And she's a girl. For all she knows you're trying to steal her boyfriend. "Discommunication, good one." She smiled at Trip, but not too long that it would seem like she was flirting with him.

Their drinks came, hot chocolate for him, strawberry soda for her. "The waitress didn't even spill half of it on the plate," Trip said seriously. "This place is quickly going to hell."

Dimitra blinked. It took her a long moment to get that he was joking. Gosh, she was so nervous. "Oh!" she blurted out with a laugh. "Right, from the time I waited you. Good one, Trip." She sipped her soda and decided to stop babbling. Small sips though, because she was still feeling ready to wee.

"Oh, Persephone sent a text. She says hi," Trip said with an upturned palm, being the messenger. "She says nice to meet you, Dimitra. You're sweet. And let's hear your idea."

Dimitra frowned, tilting her head.

"The discommunication thing. You've answered that, we'll wait for it to reach her. Speed-of-light communication, who would have thunk it would be so slow, right?" he chuckled.

Dimitra nodded. "Right! Of course. Sure, let's wait, I wanna hear her thoughts."

"Okay."

Dimitra sipped some more of her soda. It was over. Gosh, where had the entire drink gone so quickly? "Hey, Trip, lemme ask you this: You've told Persephone about the specifics of my idea, right?"

"Yes…" Trip sighed. "Trust me, there is no way to tell your girlfriend what a great idea you've come across that involves another woman. But after the initial argument, we've got nothing else to do really, we argue all the time, we spoke calmly and we actually considered it."

Dimitra sucked air. "Tsk, Trip, sorry if I caused something-"

Trip raised his palm. "Really, it's fine. I wouldn't have brought it up to Persephone if I didn't know her that well, and if we didn't trust each other."

Dimitra breathed deep, in and out again through her nose. "Good. That's good." She tapped the table. It thought she wanted to order another soda, sensing that she was done with the glass, but she swiped it away.

"What you said just earlier, it's a good argument. That's what we wanted to hear, because you didn't tell me those things last time," Trip said.

Dimitra noticed he hadn't touched his chocolate drink. Huh. He must have been nervous too. But sadly, that didn't make her feel any better. "Yeah…" she sighed, slouching forward. "I've been looking for a good thesis subject for months now, and the professor was on my ass about it because he wanted to start some other project and he can't supervise me if I take too long, and this came up! So, yeah." She nodded, her eyes up towards the afterburner sunset. "Here I am, asking you both if you want me to become your surrogate sexual partner and allow me to write about it."

Trip looked up as well.

"Names changed, of course," Dimitra added.

"Of course," Trip shrugged, clearing his throat.

Dimitra tapped the table. This discommunication was killing her. She could see how it would completely kill the mood for a girl. Well, she didn't know about Persephone specifically, but in her place, Dimitra would be turned off by it, no matter how much she wanted to do it with her boyfriend.

Trip forced a smile at her, waiting as well. He still hadn't touched his chocolate.

Dimitra put her forehead on the table. "God, the wait is killing me… I'm so anxious to hear Persephone's answer."

Trip chuckled. "Trust me, I know."

He was such a patient man. Dimitra liked that about him. His fingers caressed the curves of his cup.

Finally, he jerked up, rattling the chocolate cup. He perked up, meeting Dimitra's eyes. "Let me put you through to this, so we can both hear it."

He sent a group chat request and Dimitra immediately slapped 'accept' on her veil.

"Dimitra," Persephone said on the recorded message. Her voice was soft, kind. Dimitra could easily imagine her being her friend. "I thought about it. It does sound insane, and we barely know you. But that's fixable, right? Let's just say I'm open to it, because I love Trip so much and I know he's suffering with our situation. I think we should call tonight a date and let's get to know each other better, alright?"

Dimitra covered her mouth, and squealed something incoherent. "Yes! Of course, let's do this," she said and her voice was now going to Persephone as well, albeit with the dreaded delay.

Trip breathed out deep and met her eyes. He looked hopeful. He smiled and said, "Well, Dimitra. Tell me more about yourself." Then he picked up his hot chocolate and drank some.

CHAPTER EIGHT

Their intercourse was slow, but steady. Persephone went on about her day, and every few minutes, her comm chirped and there was a text from Dimitra. They added each other online and Trip footed the bill for Dimitra's subscription. Beaming messages into the outer reaches of the solar system wasn't exactly covered in your usual cellphone plan. Dimitra was very thorough, wanting to learn all about them.

"Tell me if you're tired or anything. 'Cause I have more questions."

"To be honest, I like getting this off my chest. You know, having someone to talk to about my relationship that isn't my stupid little sister."

"You don't talk to her about Trip?"

"Oh, we do. But her response is usually a snarky comment or

something that makes me wanna strangle her. She's too young anyway, what does she know?"

"I see. And how about other girlfriends? Aboard the ship, I mean."

"Nope."

"Touchy subject? It's okay if you don't wanna tell me."

"It is kinda touchy, yes. But there's not much to say. I don't really have any friends up here. We used to hang out with a couple of girls back when we were little, but as soon as they were twenty or so the AI had them pair up and make a couple of babies. It's all planned and everything, trust the machine. Whooey sounds, you know?"

"I see. That must have been hard, Persephone. I'm sorry you grew apart."

"Yeah, pretty much. They have their families now, their husbands, their babies. We stumbled on each other with Suzie a few months ago, but we really had nothing to say apart from tickling the baby she was holding."

"Since we're on the subject, and I know it's a touchy one, don't you want to make a family?"

"You mean since I'm in a relationship where it can't

physically happen? Yes, I do. But not yet, you know? I'm still too young. I was glad the AI didn't choose me to breed, I would have to obey, and I'll tell you, it would SUCK."

"That's probably why it didn't choose you. They're very good at picking up behavioral patterns like that, especially in a controlled environment."

"That's one way to call our tin can where our every fart is being monitored and recycled."

"I know. It sucks that you didn't have a choice in the matter."

"It is what it is. I guess I think too much. I watched Suzie, the one with the baby, and she was always so aloof. Never arguing the bigger stuff, she just lived her life, limited as it is in here. It never bothered her that she would never go anywhere else that the ship, that she wouldn't meet anyone else that wasn't still in his diapers."

"I get it. Well, inquiring minds are needed for the colony, it just sucks to be in the middle of the relay chain."

"Exactly! It's a relay race, and I'm stuck in the second spot. My entire purpose in life is to receive the baton and pass it on to the next girl, because the colony is all that matters. Nothing I do has any meaning whatsoever. Nothing. And nobody cares what I do as long as I don't fumble and drop the baton."

"Do you talk to Trip about these things?"

"I used to. He's a good conversationalist, but the nihilism of these discussions made us both depressed, so I just stopped, I guess."

"Persephone, that's so sad. I'm sorry."

"It's not your fault, Dimitra. It's nobody's. That's the problem, I can't be mad at anyone. I just drew the short straw in life."

"Tell me about something fun aboard the ship."

"Fun… Well, the aquafarms are fun. There are so many smells, and the plants, there are even some flowers! One day I got to pick one, a farmer let me have it. I put it in water but it only survived for a couple of days, tops. Then it withered and died so I recycled it."

"Do you have that part of the ship where there's no gravity?"

"Oh, yeah! In the middle shaft. It rotates, but the middle makes a smaller arc so it never gets to push you to the floor. You can freefall in the middle, it's lots of fun! But it made me lose my breakfast the last time I tried it. It's been years. Actually, it was when I used to hang out with the girls. Time flies, even in here."

"Why don't you try doing that again? The freefall. I think it would be fun, the way you described it."

"Nah… It's silly, kids' stuff."

"Well, do it for me. I've never done it, I'm stuck in a gravity well!"

"What do you mean, do it for you?"

"Well… Since I'm offering to be your surrogate, you can get a taste of what it'll be like the other way around. My whole idea was for us to link up and you giving me instructions on what you wanna do, and I'll perform it in the real. So, why not try it out the other way? I'd like you to go to the central shaft and experience the freefall for me, and record the whole thing so I can enjoy it all the way back on Earth."

"You, lady, are quite pushy."

"I just think it would be fun for the both of us."

"Oh, it's okay. I like you. Fine, Dimitra. I'll do the silly thing, but only because you didn't get to play around in zero-g when you were a kid."

"Yay!"

CHAPTER NINE

"Oh my god, this is amazing!" Dimitra kept watching and rewatching the freefall video. She leaned with her back on her bed and kept her head in the air, imagining what it was like to fall in microgravity.

Persephone giggled. "Okay, it was fun, I'll admit that. I had forgotten how awesome it was. Thank you for insisting."

"Wow…" Dimitra texted and then stood up, awaiting the lag. She went to her computer and fired up her text editor. She typed down some of her notes, the getting acquainted part, the experience she just had. She wanted to get it down quick, now that it was fresh in her mind. The research could take you anywhere, and even if it didn't make the final cut, she herself wanted to remember it.

Dimitra was old school when it came to writing things down. Everybody pretty much recorded holos these days, which could be translated to any other medium, including text, and any language in the world. But she was good with words and she liked writing things down.

It was a habit from her mother, she always wrote things. Poems, shopping lists, little notes for her, even just a post-it on her lunch tupper. Dimitra never threw them away and when she left the house she realized she had tons of them in various places. She still wasn’t capable of throwing them away so she just put them in more boxes and left them in the bottom of a cupboard.

"How come you’ve only moved to the city just now? Didn’t you study there?" Persephone asked.

"Well, it was too expensive so I just tele-educated. The courses were offered in VR by the university, they even got me a little drone to act as my avatar during class. Oh, hey, pretty much like what we’re talking about."

She sent her reply and went back to writing. Those little interruptions every eight or ten minutes had become a habit of hers. Like a Pavlovian response, she awaited Persephone's reply simply by her internal clock. She should ask Trip if it was the same to him. Actually, why not do it now?

"Hey, Trip, are you doing the same as me? Jerking up every ten minutes or so awaiting Persephone's text?"

"Hah! Yeah. All the time, Dimitra. It's hard-wired in me by now. Good luck kicking that habit."

"Are you talking to her right now as well?"

"We don't talk that often nowadays. She just mentioned she's chatting with you, that's all."

There was sorrow coming in through Trip's response, she could feel it. But she wasn't there to fix their relationship, only to address the problem and analyse things.

"Okay. We're talking about you, by the way, so don't be alarmed when you start sneezing or anything."

"Superstitious, much? Heh. I get it, girl talk. It's fine by me, as long as she doesn't tell you the thing."

"What thing?"

"I'm not telling you!"

Dimitra smiled and went back to writing. Her proposal was coming along nicely, and her professor wanted it ASAP, so that was good.

Persephone's reply finally came back. "And you chose this subject? Also, I wouldn't know about all that, but I guess living in the city is expensive, right? I mean, Trip always complains about the insane rent and how he can't miss a single paycheck."

"I didn't choose this specifically, nobody did. I already told you that this is virgin territory. Heh, get it? Virgin? 'Cause we're about to have sex and everything. Wow, I'm joking about boning your boyfriend, somebody shut me up now. Back on topic, yeah, the city is insanely expensive. I couldn't come study here in person, and my entire class is graduated now, so that's why I don't know anyone. I guess it would have been better to come for the last term, at least? Get a sense of the place, get to know people? But what's done is done, and here we are, and I'm all alone in the big city with a thesis deadline."

Dimitra stood up and went for a pee, and then opened her fridge. There was precious little in there, she needed to go to the grocery store. She grabbed a half-eaten yogurt and sat back in bed, kicking her shorts off. She always liked staying with her underwear on the bed, and it was warm enough.

"Trust me, I've went through the entire ladder of phases in my mind already. Jealously, anger, mistrust, envy, and whatever the hell the others are, I felt them like pouring hot oil. I'm okay with it, Dimitra. I wouldn't have asked to meet you if I wasn't. Of course I have my doubts, but we'll see. As for the whole city thing, yeah, that sucks. I guess we're all alone in our own way, despite being around so many people."

"Well put, Persephone! I'm so stealing that line, it's going in my paper." She finished the yogurt and licked the foil and the inside walls.

"Oh, that's me! Witty. Sarcastic. Quotable. That's probably why nobody can stand me who isn't a blood relation."

"Well, who cares? I like you, I feel we could hang out anytime. And witty is good for my thesis, so snark away, girl." Dimitra took a nap. She woke up from the chirpy noise, struggling to keep her one eyelid open.

"Hey, I know I said I was okay with the whole thing, but you won't do anything without telling me, right? I mean, with Trip. You know, making out or whatever."

Okay, that woke her up. Dimitra sat up and composed her message. "Persephone, of course not. Look, everything goes through you. I'm a conduit, a medium. You're the fucking ghost that controls me. Whatever you say, happens. I'll only fill in the gaps for the lag, but that will happen after I get a feel of what you wanted to do at any given moment. Don't worry, alright?"

She bit her nails as she awaited the reply. God, this lag was killing her. Persephone could back out, and she had every right to. She could simply say, 'nope, I want this to stop,' and her entire paper would be gone. Sure, she might try and find other couples in a similar situation. But she genuinely liked those two, and she didn't thing she could connect with some random people after this. Also, there weren't any other couples in an increasing-distance relationship. They had all taken the natural route and broken up. Trip and Persephone were outliers in this regard, which means, research-worthy.

Persephone responded and Dimitra yelped, dropping her phone under the bed. She shuffled around, felt her way under the bed, grunted, found her phone and checked the message in a hurry. "Good. I just wanted you to say it. Not that I could do anything to stop you in case you wanted to… Anyway, that's just crazy-me talking, ignore it. You've given me no indication of that sort of subterfuge. So, how will we do this thing? Will it be like sexting? Me in your ears, what? I haven't thought of that."

Dimitra breathed in deep. They were good to go, that was all that mattered. She leaned back on the bed and wrote her reply. "I have thought about it a bit. Let's practice now, the two of us. I'm in my bed, in my panties. Say that it's you and Trip comes along, comes home. That's the scenario. Let's try it out, tell me what you want me to do."

Dimitra waited for her instructions, and it was kinda getting her worked up. She sat back comfortably and put her pillow between her legs, getting the corner of it squeezed tight and rubbing on her panties. She was getting wet by the whole idea, that of receiving instructions. It was exciting!

"Well… Okay, I want you to sit on a sexy pose, wait for him to come home from work. That's my sexual fantasy, how lame is that? Just be there at home, waiting for my boyfriend to come home from work. I never had that."

Dimitra sat in a sexy pose, or at least something she thought would look sexy. Nobody could see her but it wouldn't hurt to be thorough. Plus, it was seriously getting her in the mood, she started to touch the area and rub her intimates. "Okay, I had a thought. Let's not say, 'I want you to do this and that.' Let's try and make the whole experience more transparent. I'm not in the middle, you are alone with Trip. So, let's try and rephrase that to, 'I'm sitting in a sexy pose, waiting for Trip to come home from work.' And we have a three-way communication open, we can both hear you, but whatever you say you're doing, I go ahead and do it for you. Does that make sense?"

Dimitra breathed in deep. This was starting to take shape, they were just working out the kinks.

Heh, the kinks. Funny. But that made it horrifying. It was one thing to say you were gonna do it, and another to actually go ahead and do it.

Persephone's message came back, pushing her out of her train of thought. "I'm alone, in bed, waiting for Trip. The bed is messed up, it's not neat. This isn't a special occasion, it's just a random day and I'm going to surprise my boyfriend with my impulsiveness. I sit on the bed on my side, looking all sexy with my hair drenched all over the pillow and my panties shaping my ass."

Oh-kay. That was much better. "Doing it. Go on."

Dimitra sat as she instructed. She had shorter hair than Persephone, she had seen her profile pictures, but that wasn't the point. She tried to set the scene as she said so and debated one last thing with herself. "We are gonna do it in the end, might as well show it all today." She opened up the camera from her eye-implants, giving Persephone access.

Persephone responded with audio. Her voice was soft, sultry. She was breathing deeply, and Dimitra was sure that she was doing the same thing up in her bunk. "Oh, I like the view, Dimitra! Nice panties, I like the print. I don't do lace either. We don't have the printing materials to spare for such things. Anyway, where was I? Am I gonna play the whole thing out, as if Trip was there? I guess so. Mmm. I'm waiting for Trip, and I hear him coming up the elevator. I get all worked up, rub myself a bit, getting the landing strip ready, you know. He opens the door, looks around, seems me and smiles wide, his eyes gleaming. I say, 'What?' with an innocent expression and turn over to show him the goods. He kicks off his shoes and hops into bed with me, taking his shirt off, fumbling with the buttons. I can't act all aloof anymore so I help him take it off, he lifts up his arms and I pull the shirt off of him. I touch his chest and reach in and take a bite of his pecks."

Dimitra acted the whole thing by herself, pretending Trip was there. She was getting seriously horny by now, and it was actually fun. As she waited for Persephone to speak to her again, she thought about what she would actually do in this situation to cover up the lag. Well, she'd keep teasing his body and nibbling him, so she pretended to do just that. She couldn't imagine Trip on that role, she didn't know him that well, so she casted George in his place, one of her old boyfriends who had a similar build with him.

"I bite him, he pushes me back, I keep nibbling at him. We kiss passionately, my tongue rolling around with his. Our hands wander over our bodies, I press my chest onto his. Grab my ass, Trip, and push me down on the bed. I yelp with excitement and he pushes me on my back, kissing me on my belly. He draws a line of kisses down to my panties, and he kisses me all over the place, my inner thighs, my butt, my cunt. He pulls my feet up and takes off my panties. He takes off his pants and I grab his erection, jerking him off for a while."

Dimitra mimicked the entire thing. She was too horny to feel silly, and this was academic research, dammit! She jerked off the air, pretending her ex-boyfriend was there. That wasn't hard to do, she remembered having to help him get up quite a few times, actually. And Persephone's voice in her ear, it was so damn hot. And the feeling of someone guiding you, that surrender of control…

Oh, Dimitra was sure she was gonna enjoy this project.

"I spread my legs, lick my lips. 'Come on, baby, I want you,' I say to him and he comes on top of me, aiming towards my centre. I help guide him in and he pushes inside. But he has remembered to put on a condom before sticking it inside me, right Dimitra? Right, too horny now, moving on. He takes me, I can feel him deep inside me. I kiss him, grab his shoulders, dig in my nails in his skin as he fucks me, wrap my legs around him. I scream, 'Yes, fuck me, yeah, Trip!' I pull his face to mine and kiss him again, getting my tongue all over his. I grind my waist on his body, push up with my legs, and he fucks me harder. I grab his head, lean into his ear and breathe hard in it as I come, letting him hear everything, feel everything, the way he made me reach orgasm."

Dimitra acted the entire thing, rubbing herself with one hand all the way. "Wow!" she panted, falling back on her bed. "I'm seeing stars on the ceiling, let me get my breathing under control for a minute, Persephone. Whoo."

Persephone's voice came back and Dimitra could hear the grin on her face. "Yeap. Did you really come? I did. Haaa… Yes, I do enjoy this. Thanks for opening up the camera and the audio, it really helped put me in the mood. I can only imagine how it will be with the actual Trip around."

Dimitra's chest had stopped heaving, but she remained in bed, sweaty and enjoying the relaxation after a good wank. She giggled, "Oh yeah. I sure did. It was gooood."

CHAPTER TEN

Over the next week, Dimitra and Persephone did everything together. They went grocery shopping, they did chores together, which Persephone found fascinating 'cause the drones on the ship did all that stuff if you didn't want to yourself. It was funny how back on Earth people had everything they could possibly wish for and still they had to do menial things like that.

She chose to mop the ship. It was her home, and she took good care of it. Nobody forced her, if left unattended, some drone would sweep by at some point and do the task. But humans go stir-crazy if they don't do things to occupy their minds, which was a severe problem in generation ships.

And then, they went shopping for clothes. For their date with Trip. Persephone had no idea why she was so anxious about what to wear, it wasn't like she would wear it herself. And their body types were not exactly the same, so they had to work together, find something that Persephone would like, but that would also fit Dimitra. They both took it as a challenge rather than a problem. "Forget about the distance. Think of what you'd wear," Persephone said and spread out a few frilly tops.

"No on the frills, Dimitra."

"Okay! How about simple tops that hug the waist and… you know. Have a modest décolletage, enough to draw in the gaze, not too slutty. I think those two will fit me nicely. Do you like them?"

Persephone did. So they tried them on, looked at themselves on the mirror and tried on a few skirts as well. They came up to their knee, but they went well with the tops. So, that was it. Clothing, check.

"Where will we go for our date?" Dimitra asked, carrying the shopping bags down the mall.

"At the café," Persephone responded. They spoke in both text and audio alternatively, and the camera was on the whole time. Dimitra seemed to have gotten over her prudeness after the night they had together and she was streaming the whole time, only to Persephone of course.

Dimitra darted off into the bathroom. "Hey, there are people here, watch where you aim those eyes!" Persephone complained, covering up the far too raw videostream of a girl pooping back on Earth.

"Sorry," Dimitra winced. "I had to go fast."

Persephone bit her lip. She had a naughty idea all of a sudden. It was like a game of 'Simon Says,' after all, wasn't it? She pressed to record an audio message, thought better of it and then cancelled it. Then she hopped up to her feet, checked that the door to her quarters was locked, and she started recording again. "I'm in the public bathroom, excited about my new clothes for my date. I can't wait for Saturday night and I slide my hand in my panties, feeling it around. I'm wet and I imagine how he'll react when he sees me up close, how we'll have a nice dinner together and then how he'll rip them off me back at his place."

Persephone regretted it as soon as she sent it, but the deed was done. The message was sent, and now she had to wait for the damn lag before she could see if Dimitra would go ahead. She might just tell her to piss off. It's not like they had a contract or anything. There were limits to what a person would agree to do anyway, and an impromptu wank in a public restroom where anyone could hear was right up there on the list.

She leaned back on her bunk and bit her fingernails. Perhaps she had taken it too far. Yeah, Dimitra would just ignore her, she was late after all. The whole shopping spree had taken them far longer with all the back and forth of having to ask her if she liked this and she liked that.

Then the stream turned on again. It was Dimitra, looking downwards. Her chest was heaving, going up and down with gusto. Her hand was in her panties and she was rubbing it, with her index and middle finger, just the way she preferred it. She held her new top in her other hand, splayed all over her arm. She didn't say anything, Persephone could only hear her caught breathing and the bustle of the busy shopping mall. A couple of girls chatting in the bathroom mirror. Dimitra was rubbing it faster now.

Persephone ran off into her own bathroom, sat on the toilet and mimicked her, doing the same to herself.

CHAPTER ELEVEN

"Time for the big date," Dimitra said wearily, getting herself ready. Why was she anxious? She knew the guy already, and she had gotten to know Persephone well these past few days. Plus, the freedom of choice was exhilarating.

What do I wear? Persephone chooses it.

How much makeup? Persephone chooses it, with veto power from Dimitra. They had established that early on, Dimitra was always light on makeup, couldn't stand the feel of it on her face.

Shoes? Chosen already by Persephone, she had a thing for shoes.

"Are we ready?" Persephone asked, inspecting Dimitra's body in the mirror.

"I think we are. You know, despite the lag, I think it took me much less time to get ready for this date than I ever had before."

Persephone snorted. "Two minds are better than one."

"Two girls' minds. High five!" Dimitra said and high-fived the mirror. She giggled by herself while she waited for the lag, she knew Persephone would what she just did extremely funny.

She was at the door when she finally replied. "Haha! OMG, good one. Hadn't thought of that."

"Hey, should we let him wait?" Dimitra asked from inside the self-driving taxi.

"What? No. I can't stand to wait any longer myself."

"Okay, that's probably for the best." Dimitra smiled and looked out the window. The city was enormous around her, the tall buildings, the AR ads blasting in your face. The taxi was spamming her about some beauty centre, she could choose to get advertised at and get a 5% discount on her fare. Which Dimitra of course did every time. She had a budget for this year in the big city, and she didn't wanna blow it all off in the first month. Sure, the shopping spree they had just been on had put a dent in her electronic wallet, but it was actually clothing she would wear herself. And Persephone had a good fashion sense. Heck, she was better at being a city girl than Dimitra was.

She got taken out of her reverie by an incoming message, she tapped the button to hear it. "I take a silly selfie and send it to Trip, telling him how happy I am that I'm on my way there now." Well, she could do that. Dimitra stuck out her tongue and made a face, took a selfie and sent it to Trip. Then she frowned and texted Persephone, "Hey, I sent it as you wanted it. But perhaps you wanted me to forward it to you, so it would come from your account? I'm sorry, I don't know how to handle this…"

"No, silly, by the time we made the round-trip we'll have arrived at the café. The point was to send it on the way, it's fine. You have my permission to send selfies to my boyfriend. At least, when I ask you to."

"Cool, right. Well, almost there now. Want me to open up with something in particular?"

"I opened up the three-way channel already, it's fine. Don't overthink it, I guess?" Dimitra said in audio. "Just go with it. Tell him, 'hi baby.' We've agreed that we're gonna roleplay this to the full extent, right?"

"Got it," Dimitra nodded and pulled down her skirt. It was shorter than she was used to, but it fit her nicely and showed off her legs They took the last turn and Dimitra saw the café, illuminated in reds and yellows by the afterburner sunset. Oh god, she really hoped she wouldn't ruin this. Not so much for her thesis, but for their night together. She had become too invested in it at that point.

She got off the taxi, pulled her skirt down once again, sniffed once, checked herself on the selfie camera and went for the front balcony, where the tables were set and where Trip was waiting for her.

Her legs wobbled. "Get it together," she hissed to herself. The lines of communication were open, Persephone could see everything, hear everything. It was okay, she had gotten used to broadcasting by now. She saw Trip and her smile touched her eyes. It was genuine.

Trip waved at her and stood up, pulling the chair for her.

Dimitra took a risk and went for it. She wrapped her arms around him and kissed him lightly on the lips.

Trip froze, his eyes wide. But then he softened up and smiled back at her. "Hi, baby…" she said with much more gusto than she was going for. She cleared her throat and plopped her butt down, it was no time to practice her acting skills. She'd just be herself, but taking instructions from Persephone. "Thank you," she said, making an 'o' with her mouth while she took the seat.

Trip sat down opposite her. "Hello Persephone," he said rigidly, staring at his feet.

"Oh no, honey, come sit next to me. Let's watch the sunsets together," Dimitra nagged with a cutesy voice and wiggled her fingers for him to come. He had given her the best seat at the table, just like a gentleman should, facing the view.

"Um… Sure," Trip said and pulled up his chair next to her. He looked so uncomfortable.

"How was work, today?

Trip nodded slowly. "Good. The calculations needed a bit of

tweaking, the trajectories had a minor fault in them. We're all scrambling to get it fixed, it matters a lot for the safety of the ship."

Persephone butted in at that moment. "My poor Trip is keeping me safe. Doing all the calculations of the outer solar system debris tracking, he makes sure I'm not in any danger."

Dimitra touched his face. He was freshly-shaven, smelling of a distinct aftershave that got Dimitra's engine going. "My poor baby, keeping me safe," she squeezed her lips together, cooing at him.

Trip snorted, looking away. "You realise that doesn't make sense, logistically. I mean, you're here, yet I'm keeping you safe at the edge of the solar system? Does not compute."

Dimitra squeezed his cheek and made him turn towards her. "Just go with it, dummy." Then she kissed him on the lips, this time a bit more slurpy than the light peck she gave him earlier. Where was she getting this bravado? Dimitra needed the other guy to do the move first, always. She talked the talk, but when it was time to walk the walk she was a cheeky chicken.

Trip met her eyes and gulped, his face close to hers. "Yeah. Kept you safe again, love."

Dimitra booped his nose and leaned back. "Are we getting our usual hot chocolates?"

Trip started at that, and Dimitra knew he had noticed. This was Trip's and Persephone's drink, not Dimitra's. "Yes, I'm going all-in," she said, opening up the menu ARO. She tapped the usual for them both and sent in the order.

Trip looked flushed. It was either the reddish sky or the litres of blood from his entire body had gathered up on his face. "Uh… Yeah, thanks babe. For ordering. Our usual… I mean."

"Let's not talk about trivial matters," Dimitra said, leaning towards him again. She brushed his elbow with her tit, giving him a nice view. "It's been so long since we've spent time together. Let's enjoy the sunsets, right baby?"

Trip glanced at her chest, then turned to the sunsets. "Y-Yeah. Of course."

"I went shopping, did you notice?" Persephone said and they could both hear her. Dimitra went along and pulled up her top by the straps, pretending to straighten in.

Of course, the desired result was that her tits bobbed nicely up and down.

And this time, Trip didn't look away. "Yeah, very stylish, Persephone. I-I think they're in vogue, too? You look great. Absolutely great," he nodded like an idiot.

"Why, thank you, love," Dimitra cooed again and pulled his face to hers. She gave him a peck on the lips.

Their order came. The waitress served them with a smile and hurried away, winking at Dimitra. She took a sip. Okay, the chocolate was nice.

She didn't prefer it, she wasn't normally gonna order it by herself, but it was drinkable. It made her feel hot, and she fanned herself, showing her neck to Trip.

"Too hot?" Trip asked.

"I must be just thinking it. The sunsets feel hot, the chocolate on top is too much." Then she smiled at him. "But it's' our drink at our favourite spot, during our favourite time. So, that's what matters alone."

Persephone's voice came nagging. "Babyyy… Why are you sitting so far away from me? Hold me. Hug me."

Trip blinked. "Uh, sure." He shuffled his chair closer and touched Dimitra's side with his body. He timidly put his arm around her neck.

Dimitra leaned into him, closing her eyes. She could smell the sweet chocolate against the spicy smell of his aftershave, and she could feel the warmth of the sunsets on her face. "This is nice," she mumbled, enjoying her date. Sure, it was the weirdest date ever, but she had worse, actually.

This was nice.

"I nuzzle up in Trip's neck and enjoy the sunsets, my hand inside his," Persephone said. And her wish was Dimitra's command.

CHAPTER TWELVE

They chatted, touched each other some more, and yes, kissed. It was sweet, romantic. But Dimitra didn't know how far she should take it. The afterburner sunset was over, it was getting dark and the automatic lights turned on around the café. She bit her lip. She was mentally preparing herself for this night, but to be honest, she wanted to savour it. Then again, it was Persephone's choice. Dimitra had decided to go along with whatever she'd say.

Trip held both her hands into his. "You have no idea how much I needed this date, baby," he said softly.

Damn, he was smooth. Dimitra was not. She sniffed her nose, ended up making a sniffle of wet snot. Far from romantic. Then again, Trip was so starved of personal attention that even if she wiped a booger in his sleeve, he'd shrug it off and keep on blinking and grinning.

"I lean in, kiss him softly, then say, 'I need this to last. It was perfect. Our date was perfect. Same time next week?"

Trip blinked at her, then shook his head and broke off the embrace. Dimitra touched the side of his face and stared at his details, as if taking it all in for a faraway journey. This hadn't been something that Persephone had told her to do, but it seemed like something that a girl in her place would do.

"What are you doing?" Trip asked wearily.

"I'm taking in the details in your face. Your imperfections, the lines. I want to remember you, on my long journey back."

Triptolemus stood there in silence, looking uneasy, the way people do when someone is taking too long to take a picture of them.

Dimitra finally smirked sideways, pinched Trip's cheek and turned around to leave. She took a couple of steps, turned back and said, "Goodnight, Trip. Think of me tonight." She winked, then sauntered away.

"How was your date?" Zoe asked, hopping in place. She had the naughtiest smirk on her face.

Persephone gripped both hands on her mop, and held it as if it was a dance partnet. "Oh, you know. Dreamy," she said in that exact tone of voice.

"Did you... You know," Zoe asked, waving her hand around.

Persephone squinted at her and shook her head in puzzlement.

"Oh, you know..." Zoe made a ring with her one hand and pushed her index finger inside it with the other.

"Ah," Persephone said, realising what she meant. "No. I decided to keep it romantic, first time."

Zoe pressed her lips together, nodding slowly. "Oh, got it."

"Got what, little goblin?" Persephone snapped at her, and gripped her mop.

"You chickened out. You didn't want What's-her-name boinking your man. I understand." Zoe turned around and looked up at the monitors. They showed the outside, the stars. There was nothing much to see. It was depressing, really. A viewport might have been better, but there were no such points in the ship's hull. Only at the bridge.

Persephone raised her mop and held it like a lance at her sister. The effect was much less menacing, since the water dripped from the soggy bit. "Listen, you little green goblin. I did not chicken out. In fact, we've talked about it with Dimitra and she was ready to do it for me."

Zoe rested her head on a bit of protruding pipe and drolled. "Unh-huh. I bet she was."

Persephone let her mop hit the floor with a loud slap. Her shoulders slumped. "Even if that was the case, which it isn't, what would you have me do? It's not like I can actually intervene. You know that Trip is one ignore button away from getting rid of me, easy as pie? I have nightmares about it. It's not healthy."

"It isn't," Zoe agreed, pressing her lower lip. She stepped forward, making damn sure she stood in the spot Persephone had just cleaned.

She got a glare from her sister but she wasn't in the mood to whack her on the head.

Zoe thought about it for a moment. "Okay. I know it's hard. But

I can always introduce you to some guys. I got a friend who's into MILFs like you."

Persephone opened her eyes wide, raised her mop and threatened the little green goblin. "I'm young. I'm not a MILF!" she howled, and Zoe giggled "Too slow, old lady," and bolted out of there. Persephone chased her down the corridors, waving her mop around and dripping nanowater all over the place.

CHAPTER THIRTEEN

"Did you get the expenses approved by the uni?" Persephone asked.

Dimitra bit her lips to the side before she answered. She thought about her answer. "Yes," she lied laconically.

"Good, good…" Persephone's reply came after the lag.

Dimitra paced up and down in her little apartment. She had indeed requested money for finishing her project, but they had turned her down. The subject matter was controversial enough, her professor told her. He had liked the project and gave her the go-ahead, but no cash was coming in. And the live streaming to Persephone would add up very quickly.

But it was imperative, dammit!

Dimitra had seen how important it was for Persephone's experience. For their bond, even. Sure, the audio messages were fine, but seeing is believing. Even with a plain old cybereye camera like Dimitra's, seeing the point of view was quite immersive. She started filing up and cataloguing the recordings and their texts, all with the couple's consent, naturally. She felt too ashamed to go through their initial test, the night where Persephone lead and Dimitra followed, but she did go through a bit of the first date. That was embarrassing as hell too, but in-between all the giggling and the shame, Dimitra managed to get some notes down for their encounter. It was perhaps the most important bit of her entire paper, the first date. Sure, the first time of intimacy would be the juiciest, but the date was important as well. And, if Dimitra might say, it had been a success.

Sure, there was awkwardness, which was to be expected. And Trip took his time to acclimate, but the poor bastard didn't get a dry run or any of the hours of talking she and Persephone had already. The date smoothed out after a while, and ended so romantically!

Persephone sent a text. "I have so many things to tell you, Dimitra, that I don't know where to begin.

But mostly, I wanna say thank you, for making me this gift."

Dimitra felt tears in her eyes. She wiped them off, sniffling as she took down notes and feelings about the date, now that she had them all fresh in her mind.

"Silly girl, getting all mushy about it," she muttered, scolding herself. She finished her notes and replied to Persephone. "I'm glad you feel that way!" Smiley face, smiley face.

Then she sighed and pulled up her ebanking reports, trying to see how she could possibly make ends meet.

CHAPTER FOURTEEN

"It's time for your routine physical examination," the AI told her. Persephone groaned and got herself ready, taking a quick shower. She was in no mood to get poked and prodded again.

Zoe came in and sat on the toilet, taking a wee. "You got called?" she drolled, her face resting on her hand.

"Yeah. Got no choice. Not that I had anything else planned for today."

Zoe frowned. Persephone could see her through the foggy plastic. "But why? So they can see if you're ready for breeding? We're just cattle…" she sighed.

Persephone peeked her head out and pointed at the shampoo. "You know how it is."

"Yeah…" Zoe said and passed it on to her, then resumed her

rebellious, bored pose. The bathroom wasn't that big.

Persephone stopped the nanowater, saving it, and applied shampoo. "One of the things drilled into the colonists' minds all day and night is this: The AI is god."

Zoe blew a raspberry. But she was sitting on the toilet, panties down, so Persephone wasn't certain if it was a sound effect or a real one. Her little sister was such a piggy, sometimes.

"The AI keeps you alive. The AI will provide for you. The AI will make sure that no-matter-what, it'll get a bunch of humans, generations later, down to the target exoplanet and help them start an offworld colony."

"And what about us in-between?" Zoe complained and wiped herself clean.

"We make babies," Persephone said, freezing in shock. Not from the water, which was rather cold, but from the sudden realization. "Fuck. All my friends have given birth already. I'm next," she said, spelling out her doom.

"Can't you cheat or something?" Zoe said from across the room. Of course she let the door open, one more reason for Persephone to be freezing.

"I wouldn't dream of it, sis. It's one thing to complain about our situation, and another to actively sabotage it. I'm not crazy." Persephone rinsed herself off and toweled down.

Zoe threw her a t-shirt and panties.

Persephone put them on mechanically, as if in a trance. One foot after another, staring through the hull and straight towards empty space. "I'm twenty-three. That's the optimal fertile age. Fuck. Fuck, Zoe!" she spat out. "Fuck!"

Zoe popped her lips. "I think that's the literal problem. Fucking." She held her pants up in the air.

"Fuck!" Persephone said and snatched the pair of pants, and hobbled all over, putting them on in a hurry.

She hurried off to the medical bay, dreading of what they'd tell her.

CHAPTER FIFTEEN

Persephone got poked and prodded. The medical drone floated next to her, and said in a soothing voice, "It's just routine, don't worry. Just lie back and relax."

"Okay…" she said wearily, leaned back and stared at the forest projected on the ceiling. It had lots of detail, birds chirping, leaves moving, squirrels stealing nuts. It was perfectly made to lull the human mind and distract her. Look! Something pretty, it's moving in the bushes. Follow it with your eyes while I shove a biopsy needle up your peehole. Okay, she knew that's not where it was going in, but the sentiment was the same, and it sure felt like it.

"The tunnel is a bit tight due to being left abandoned for so long," she joked.

"It's wide enough," the medidrone said, slipping it in.

Persephone breathed out and calmed herself. She settled her hands on her chest and let the drone do its job. She was a team player, after all. Always logical, always level-headed, always ready to understand the other person's, or e-person's in this instance, point of view.

"There," the medidrone cooed softly. "All done."

Persephone stood up. She defaulted back to joking. "Will I make it, doc?"

"Of course," the medical drone said, the humour going over its head, while setting the implement in a sample collection canister. "You are healthy and young. Bone brittleness is at a low level, and your uterus' walls are looking exquisite."

"Oh, well then. At least my uterus walls look peachy."

The medical drone stared at her for a long moment, tilting its head. "As a matter of fact, they do."

"Thanks…" Persephone drolled while putting her pants back on. "You're not much for witty banter, are you?"

"I'm not," the drone shrugged.

Geez, sometimes the e-persons were so lifelike, and others, they were like… well, mindless drones.

Then again, you don't want the e-person operating on your guts to be witty, just precise and knowledgeable.

God, she felt useless. Even the silly looking drone painted with calming blue and green hues was more important than her. She was stuck, stuck in this relay race, pathetic and useless.

But at least she had nice uterus walls.

"Thank you, doc. When will I know the results of the test?"

"Oh, you'll get them on your comm when they're ready. A couple of days," the medidrone said softly.

She clapped her hands. "Great. Anything else?"

"Drink more fluids," the medidrone said with a chirp.

Persephone narrowed her eyes at it. "Will do, doc."

CHAPTER SIXTEEN

The second date was a disaster, pure and simple.

Her water heater was busted and she had to take a cold shower, her maskara ended up a mess and inside her eye making it irritated and red, and her top tore up at the seams.

"Put on the pink one," Persephone said, a little too late.

"Already on…" Dimitra huffed out and got out the door.

The self-driving taxi got confused and took her the wrong way. It took her a good ten minutes to realise it and get it to correct the route, since she hadn't been in the city that long. In retrospect, heading straight east should have been a dead giveaway.

"I'm here, sorry I'm late," she panted, getting close to Trip. She leaned in and gave him a quick kiss, but reached out too far and hit her nose on his face. "Ouch!"

Trip touched her hand and smiled. "It's okay, honey. Sit down and calm yourself, you're all tense. I didn't mind waiting a bit."

Dimitra plopped her butt down and looked over the menu. "Screw hot chocolate, I need a drink."

"Okay," Trip shrugged, the corner of his mouth raised. "I'll have a drink too, then."

"Two beers," Dimitra breathed out, going over the catalogue. "So many." She remembered that she was playing a part, so she turned on her girly whine and said, "Baby… You choose for me. You know what I like."

He stuttered. "I-I do, yes. Dark beer." He finished the order and swiped the menu away from their face.

Dimitra forced a smile on her face. She noticed that she was anxious and was leaning forward, bobbing on her arms. It was the lack of preparation. Last time, everything was perfect, her clothes, her mood, her makeup. This time it was a mess.

She was a mess.

"I touch his hand, cup it in mine and turn to see the sunsets," Persephone said.

Dimitra did exactly that, and Trip’s touch had a calming effect on her. The sunsets were almost over, she had been late. She opened up a virtual keyboard and typed up a message to Persephone. ‘I’m sorry for ruining your date, this day is not going well for me.’

"Wanna come sit next to me?" Trip asked.

"Oh, right. Sure." Dimitra carried her chair next to his and she sat down, still uneasy. She kept sniffing and pushing her hair back.

"Persephone? Are you alright?" Trip said, trying to maintain the illusion.

"Yeah," Dimitra breathed out and grabbed his hand. She scratched him a bit with her nails, she could see the red line. She tapped his hand in mockery of intimacy.

"Let's just, you know. Chat. How are you today?" he asked.

Persephone's response came in a text. "No, silly. It's fine, it happens. Don't sweat it. Let's just enjoy our date. But to be honest, I am itchy for… you know, finally doing it."

Dimitra read the message and breathed in, still holding Trip's hand with both of hers. "Why don't we take it back to your place?"

"But we just ordered…" Trip said lamely looking back, and it was obvious that he regretted his words.

"Just grab them for the road. Yeah," Dimitra nodded.

"You sure?" Trip asked, and she could tell that the question was being directed at Dimitra, not Persephone.

Dimitra leaned in and kissed him on the lips. "Yes. Yes, I am."

"Okay then." Trip swiped his paycard on the smart-table and paid for the drinks. The waitress brought them over, and he stood up and grabbed them. "We changed our mind, getting them to go."

"No problem," the waitress said and smiled wide at the both of them.

Dimitra's heart was pounding. She couldn't relax, not one tiny bit. She was in it now, she couldn't back out. And sure, things weren't going well tonight, but what the heck?

Shit happens.

"Okay, Trip, let's go to your place," Dimitra said.

She stood up. "Oh, no…" she mumbled, feeling the wetness down her thigh. "Excuse me a moment," she said and darted off to the bathroom.

"Period, right? It's fine," Persephone said.

Dimitra was in the toilet, trying to contain the damage to her pants. "I don't have a pad with me, it's two days early, dammit!" She banged her forehead on the toilet walls. "I'm sorry," she sighed, wiping herself down.

She was presentable when Persephone's reply came around. "It's fine, really. This was not meant to be our night. We'll reschedule, babe."

Dimitra froze. She had called her 'babe.' Sure, it might had been just a slip of the tongue as she was thinking about Trip, and it might not mean anything. And the point of their getting-to-know one another was to feel safe and get intimate.

But she liked that, more than she cared to admit.

Persephone spoke in their three-way channel, "It seems that I got my period. Sorry, babe, we'll meet again Wednesday?"

CHAPTER SEVENTEEN

Persephone went to the cafeteria. She rarely went there anymore, it was full of people that she preferred to avoid, honestly. She went up to the serving girl and looked down at the selection.

"Mashed potatoes, sauce, and some veggies," she said with a smile.

Persephone lifted her head and stared at her, stunned.

"What?"

"How the fuck do you remain so chipper?"

The serving girl blinked. "I'm sorry?" she asked, but she didn't seem upset about the question. She seemed more to be baffled.

"We're the same gen, right? Your name is Hara."

"Yup!" she chirped, squeezing her lips and standing on her tippy toes. "I think we were in class together, right. You're… The one with the gloomy name." She clicked her fingers.

Persephone opened her mouth but got a raised spoon in the face.

"Don't tell me. Persephone, right?" She blinked and pointed at her.

Persephone sighed. "Yeah. That's me. By the way, I want some veggies too, 'cause the medidrone thinks I don't eat healthy enough. I mean, the nerve!" she scoffed.

Hara put some mashed potatoes and started to fill a bowl with some veggies. "How come?"

"The medidrone, it doesn't even have a mouth. And it's telling me to eat healthier!"

Hara blinked at her, freezing, her big spoon held in the air. Then she shifted her expression entirely, "Oh… You're joking, now I got it." She clicked her tongue and winked, "Good one."

Persephone pressed her lips together and nodded silently. She propped herself up on the glass of the food aisle, and looked around.

Hara pushed her full plate towards her, and she accepted it. "Hey," she frowned. "What's this job like?"

Hara tapped her chin. "Well… I dunno, it's fun, I guess. You get to talk to everybody, and serve food, which is nice. The cleaning up after is not that nice, but I don't really mind."

Persephone looked around, frowning. The cafeteria wasn't full, she had chosen this time of day for this exact reason. She would agree to get her veggies, but on her own terms, dammit! She turned her face back to Hara. She was chipper, blonde. Short and insisted on smiling about everything, it seemed. "Is there an opening for the night shift?"

"Why, I think so, yes! Wanna apply?" She leaned forward, grabbing Persephone's hand. "Oh, I know! We can work together, chat with people, then gossip about them all night! Isn't that great?"

Persephone lifted her upper lip, showing her teeth in an insincere smile. "Totally" she deadpanned. "I think I need a change of scenery, or I'll go crazy."

"Oh, we can't have that. Mental health is important, keep your mind calm," Hara recited the AI's propaganda. They all knew the phrases.

Persephone grabbed a fork and started eating right there, holding her plate up. She didn't bother getting to an empty table.

"Don't you wanna sit down and eat?" Hara asked.

"I'm a rebel," Persephone said, her mouth full of healthy, nutritional veggies. Veggies that would prepare her body for the single use that she was good for.

She knew it was coming. Her biological clock was ticking, and she was certain that the AI had a literal countdown for her somewhere in its subroutines. She tried to push the 'Grand Plan' from her mind for a moment, and try to live in the there and now.

"Is it good?" Hara asked, looking expectant. She looked so dorky with her little hat.

"Yeah. Better than the edible crap I was getting from the store."

Hara smiled and leaned in over the counter. She spoke in a conspiratorial tone, "When you get on the shift with me, we'll be able to lick the pot afterwards. It's the best part," she said and nodded.

"I bet," Persephone snorted.

"I tell you, it's the best part of the job."

Persephone froze with her fork in the air and turned to examine her. "You're fucking serious."

"I am!" Hara squealed with a cute shrug.

CHAPTER EIGHTEEN

"What do you mean, you broke up?" Dimitra all but screamed in the message. Argh! This lag was killing her. She paced up and down her room. She needed to iron her clothes but her hands were trembling. After a couple of attempts and a burned finger she pushed the damn chore for tomorrow.

She stuck her finger in her mouth and sat on her chair, frowning.

The thought hadn't even occurred to her. Those two bozos could simply break up, and poof, her thesis was gone. And she had already invested so much time and effort into it. Heck, it wasn't even salvageable at this point, there was no conclusion, no information to extract. Trip and Persephone had allegedly broken up, and now she was thoroughly fucked.

She couldn't wait for the lag, she called up Trip. As soon as he picked up, she went straight into crazy-chick mode. "Hey, what the fuck is Persephone telling me? You guys broke up? What the hell, dude?"

"Dimitra, calm down," Trip said on the phone. He had repeated the same thing a couple of times now.

"Don't tell me to calm down!" she squealed at him. "Answer me."

"I'm trying to. Yes, we had a fight. It happens way too often, I'm afraid," Trip sighed.

"You didn't tell me about the fighting during the interview," Dimitra protested.

"Yeah…" He trailed off and sounded ponderous. "We… Look, we get into fights all the time. We say mean things, we break up, block each other, ignore each other's calls… It's what you do when you're far away, you know?"

Dimitra scrunched up her nose and propped up the phone on her desk. She gestured with both hands, touching thumb and index finger. "Trip. My dear boy, Triptolemus. If you guys break up, I'm fucked. I'm not trying to be selfish here, I actually am bummed out that you had a fight. But I stuck my neck out with you two and now you're telling me, you're just done? Finito?"

"Finito," Trip agreed with a deep sigh.

"No! No finito. No-no-no, man. You get on that phone, and you call her up, and you say you're sorry and you're an idiot and that you want her back and that you love her from here all the way to the stars, got it?"

There was a pause.

"Trip. Fucking answer me." Dimitra was looming over the phone on the desk, feeling her veins ready to pop out of her forehead.

A grumble and another pause. "Dimitra, she's gonna get pregnant," he said with a pain evident in his voice.

Dimitra deflated on the chair. She blinked. "Oh, fuck." She rubbed her eyes. "Oh, man, I'm sorry."

"Yeah…" Trip said, acting all brave and strong, but his voice broke.

Dimitra didn't know what to say. "D-Do you need a friend? Want me to come over, talk it through?" she stuttered.

Another pause. She could imagine Trip looking away into the distance, a bit upwards. She had seen him do that when he was pensive, like staring at the sunsets. He swallowed. "Thanks. Uh… Perhaps tomorrow. I appreciate it, really."

He hung up.

Dimitra sat there blinking. There she was, thinking about her stupid thesis when they had actual, adult problems to deal with. A life! She would bring a life into this world. Okay, into the generation ship, but still. Her friend, her confidante. She had mentioned the trips to the doctor and the medical exams but it hadn't sunk in apparently. Dimitra knew that the entire generation aboard the ship was expected to breed, but the reality was that she hadn't really understood the consequences.

Persephone's message finally came through. "Sweetie, I need to tell you what happened. It's bad. Do you have the time?"

Dimitra smiled bitterly and sent a message back. "Of course, dear. I'm here, tell me everything."

CHAPTER NINETEEN

Papers slammed into Dimitra's face. "You're the one who asked for this!" the man said, after having thrown the bunch at her.

She flinched, but she didn't look away. Nor did she complain. She just stood there, taking the heat. "Yes, I did, professor."

The man turned in his chair. It was big and leather and important, and he was a man who had important things to do in his important office at the top of the university. He looked out of the window, up towards the gathering sunsets.

There was silence for a minute. Dimitra didn't dare end it.

The professor turned back towards her and straightened his tie. "I..." he said, gripping the edges of his dark-wooden desk, "didn't want this. But you insisted, and then I trusted you, so I sold this to the higher-ups. They think it's brilliant, and they want it done." He shook his head, "Heavens knows why." He pointed a finger at her. "So, you, will have to find a way to make this whole deal work."

"I-I don't think that's possible now, sir. I mean, if the couple breaks up, what could I possibly-"

He slammed his hand on the desk, making her flinch. "You are the who brought this to me. Now see to it."

She nodded, it was almost a bow. "Yes, sir."

He waved his hand in a dismissing gesture, so Dimitra turned away and started to leave. Then she stopped. "Professor?" she asked, her hand on the door handle.

"Yes?" he asked, his patience obviously wearing thin.

"I stand by it," she said, raising her chin a fraction of a centimetre.

"Stand by what?" he snapped at her.

"Stand by the fact that it's worthwhile anthropological research, sir. It can help people, especially as we expand more into outer colonies."

He snorted, turning his face away. "Don't try to justify your kinks with big talk, you academic whore."

And with that happy thought, she walked out of the university.

CHAPTER TWENTY

"I want more of the red sauce," the annoying little cunt said. She was a blonde with an upturned nose. Or, perhaps that was her constantly upturned head looking down on people.

Persephone eyed her. Hard. Then she stuck her big spoon inside the red sludge and poured some more red sauce on the annoying little cunt's plate. She forced a smile and made it as fake as possible. "There. Happy now?"

"I am. But I will file a complaint next time if there's the same injustice," she said, rolling her shoulder.

Persephone's eyes widened. She gripped the edge of the food warmer. "Injustice? Pick up a history book once in your life, you miserable-"

"Persephone," Hara said calmly, squeezing her shoulder. "You're doing it again."

Persephone panted and turned to look at her. "I am," she agreed, and rubbed her nose with a sniff.

Hara winced and her voice went up a few octaves. "Well, mayyybe this job isn't the best fit for you…" She corrected immediately. "Not that I don't like working with you, but you get too worked up about all the people."

"They keep asking for food!" Persephone shouted and she realized how stupid it sounded on her own as soon as it left her lips.

"Yeah…" Hara pressed her lower lip. "It's kinda the whole reason for coming here. You know, socialize, have somewhere to eat." She chuckled. "I mean, they're not coming for the cuisine, that's for sure." She held up her spoon in one hand, and twiddled a knife in the other.

Persephone snorted at that. "Yeah…" She picked up a big sack of red sludge with a grunt and held it up on the counter. "I still don't get what the big deal is."

Hara slashed the side of the sack and placed the knife at its proper place, held tight on a magnetic slot. She shrugged, drolling her words. "You know… Bring someone over. Meet someone, that's always exciting! Even having dinner with some family, that makes it worth it." She propped herself up on her arms and looked up, daydreaming.

"What a LOAD OF CRAP, HARA," Persephone shouted in the chipper girl's face and started to pour the next batch of sludge in the warmer.

Hara poked Persephone's tit with her spoon. "Hey, I have an idea. Why don't you try it out yourself?"

"Try what?" Persephone frowned, controlling the flow of the sludge.

"Invite someone over. Try it out. See what the fuss is about." Hara suddenly broke into a wide smile. "Hey, that rhymed!"

Persephone squeezed the sack and emptied out the sludge. "I don't really have anyone," she said with a tiny voice.

"Come on, sure you do! You can invite your sister, or that boyfriend you never talk about, right?" Hara said, blinking furiously like a person on drugs.

"I don't wanna talk about it," Persephone said in the tone of voice of someone who has said the same thing a million times already and she doesn't wanna talk about it, dammit!

Hara put her hands up in surrender while still holding the spoon, spreading food on the side wall. She didn't seem to notice. "Okay, okay. Jeez. Just, invite someone. Have people serve you food. Sit beside the windows, watch the view of the stars."

"It's not a real window," Persephone drolled, rolling up the empty sack. "It's a big monitor showing us the outside, which is a starry night. Always. The same. Day in, day out. Stars."

Hara's voice pitched higher. "Some find that romantic, you know."

"Only the dumb ones," Persephone said, leaning into Hara's face.

Hara frowned. "I like it," she said quietly.

Persephone bit her lip and looked away. She had done it again, mocking and insulting the person who had spent two days trying to be her friend. Why was she being such a bitch? Sure, it was the fight with Trip. And the fact that her best friend was on the other side of the solar system. Oh, and by the way, that same best friend was only hanging around because her and Trip's unusual relationship circumstances. If that was gone, then she'd be gone too. And Persephone realized that she didn't want her gone from her life.

Not now.

Not when she'd be asked to-

Not now.

Gosh, she was terrified of losing Dimitra. Yes, she cared about losing Trip equally bad, but usually losing a boyfriend didn't mean you lost a girlfriend as well. Well, not unless said boyfriend had slept with said girlfriend, but in their case that was the desired result.

What a mess.

She turned back to Hara who was going through the motions quietly next to her, cleaning up the mess they made on the counters. Sludge-pouring was not a clean affair, that much was certain. "Hara, I'm sorry. I didn't mean to call you dumb, and I didn't mean to call the cafeteria dumb."

Hara turned back to her, hands held together on her chest. "That mean you'll try it out?" Her eyes were wide, expectant.

Persephone sighed. "Yes. Yes, I'll invite someone to the

cafeteria. Why the fuck not?" she said, throwing her arms in the air.

CHAPTER TWENTY-ONE

Dimitra went for a jog. She wanted to say that it was her habit, but to be honest, she never went jogging. Not even back at her hometown, where there was plenty of open space and lovely nature to run around in.

She ran, pacing herself. She knew she was a bit out of shape and the last thing she needed was a cramp or something. No, she was self-conscious enough to try and burn some calories, but not force herself too much at the same time. She panted, stopped and took a sip of her water. The city had a nice park, and there were joggers running up and down, it was almost crowded. Of course, like everything, people turned this simple act into a race and a mating ritual. There was a guy in his fifties over there, trying to prove to the young ladies that he still got it. There was a woman in her thirties, shocked by the discovery of drooping skin and other bits. And those two girls in their twenties, sharing their jog online, with a selfie drone following them as they giggled and made faces. Actually, of the three groups, the last one was the one who seemed to be having the most fun of them all. Frivolous, sure. But that's how they had been raised, and this was a healthy exercise. So what if they minded their Agora followers and the reactions they got in the mean time?

Dimitra didn't have any followers. Just some people from back in the town, who she grouped into a category that didn't get her big city updates. Last thing she needed was for everyone to be gossiping about her back home.

And now? With her thesis? Now that was juicy gossip.

She could almost hear their whispers. An academic whore.

Even her professor had seen it like that. Not the one who picked up her thesis, but another one, one who she used to respect after reading all of his books. He actually told her to find an easier way to whore herself, no need to make such a big deal out of it.

Nasty comments. That's what she needed to get out of her head.

Dimitra pressed her lips together and started running again. She ran past the mid-life crisis guy, past the sagging tits lady, and past the selfie girlfriends and kept on running. She jumped in place and snatched the selfie drone from midair.

The two girls cried out, "Hey! That's ours."

Dimitra didn't care. "I'll give it back next round," she shouted and darted off. She turned the selfie drone towards her face, holding it before her as she would a pet. The camera was on her, recording her every move.

"I'm Dimitra," she said to the foreign followers, still running. She was exerting herself, getting sweaty and reddish and blotchy. She wasn't pretty, she knew that. "I'm an academic whore," she said to everyone who was listening. She still ran, almost having finished the round and getting close to the spot where she started from. She felt like dying, her legs hurt. Heck, she hadn't ran this much since she was a kid. She always used to run everywhere. Running is fun, that's why kids do it every chance they get. Adults forget about it sometimes. And sure, they take up jogging, and get the endorphins and they remember that it feels like fun.

But they overcomplicate it in the process. It's no longer just them, their pair of legs and the open road. It's sports bras and waterproof eyeliner and electrolytes and showing off to the ladies and the gents and checking to see if your tits are still saggy and fitness counters and broadcasting it all to anyone who cares to watch.

Dimitra felt she was gonna collapse. She was completely out of shape, she couldn't even handle one lap. Panting, she forced herself to keep going. She had her mouth open, panting like a bitch. She didn't look pretty. She kept the selfie drone up, aimed at herself. She couldn't see the girls' followers reactions and comments. She didn't have instant feedback on her actions, on her stupidity.

She was just a girl trying to prove to herself that she could do it, dammit!

She forced her leg to move forward, then the other, then repeated the motion. They burned, her calves, her thigh muscles, her whatever they were called down below. She could see the finish line, though.

It was the line she had started from, and all she needed was like thirty more metres and she would prove to herself she could do it. Twenty. Fifteen. Her legs didn't move.

She fell via momentum alone for the last few metres and collapsed on the finish line, the selfie drone tumbling out of her hand and on the ground.

The mid-life crisis came leaning over her, worried. "Are you okay, miss?" He fanned some air into her face.

The saggy tits lady unstrapped Dimitra's water bottle from her calf and splashed some on her face. "That feels nice..." she mumbled, her eyes unfocused.

From somewhere next to her, she head the piercing shrieks of the selfie girls. They picked up their drone and threw it in the air. It came crashing down on the ground, one of the propellers bent. It was unable to maintain its balance.

"I'm sorry. I'll pay for it," Dimitra mumbled.

"What? No, it's fine, girl! You got us like, a thousand shares," one of the selfie girls said, scrolling through her feed in her veil. "They're calling you the academic whore."

"Good," Dimitra snorted and let her head fall back onto the ground.

Immobility. It felt glorious.

CHAPTER TWENTY-TWO

Hara scrunched up her nose and looked around the cafeteria. "This feels weird."

"Hey, you're the one who told me to invite someone over and hang out."

Hara whined. "Yes, I meant someone from the ship. Not from Earth!"

Persephone leaned forward and touched her hand. "It's no big deal, trust me. You get the hang of it. Just wait for the lag, and then just roll with it. It's like theatre, someone feeding you the lines."

"Oh! Like acting! I can do that," Hara perked up.

They let a minute pass in silence, and it was awkward for the both of them. Then Hara's eyes opened up to some unseen and unheard message, and she smiled. She made a show of looking around, as if having just arrived there. "Well, this place is interesting. Ironic to think that this cafe is on the other end of the afterburner sunset we see from down here."

Persephone smiled. "I'm so glad you could make it."

Hara gave her a warm smile. "Anything for you, dear."

Persephone bit her lip and looked away. "I wanted to speak to you. Tell you about what happened."

"I'm listening."

"Dimitra, I was so afraid that I was gonna lose you too. I mean, of course my heart breaks when I think of me and Trip, but you came in my life so suddenly, and we clicked, just like that." She snapped her fingers.

"I'm not going anywhere," Hara said, acting as Dimitra.

Persephone shut her eyes and relaxed. "That's awesome."

"Come on. Girl talk. Tell me what happened," Dimitra said.

Then Persephone went on a winding explanation of why they fought, what Trip said, what he didn't say, how it related to past fights they've had, how it made her feel, how the fact that he wasn't getting her made her feel, and generally a lot of nuance and detail.

When she was finally done, both their drinks were empty and Hara was sucking her straw making annoying sounds. That wasn't Dimitra, that was Hara's habit, but Persephone tried to ignore it. She was, after all, filling in for her bestie. And she couldn't say no, since she was the one who told her to do this. Killing two birds with one stone, that was Persephone. Efficient. But still worthless.

Hara had a deep frown on her face. It was obvious that she was digesting it all, but to be honest,

Persephone only cared for Dimitra's opinion. "Hmm..." she said, tapping her lower lip. "There is a way to fix this. I mean, a way to accommodate all parties, both your duty to the colony and Trip's role as your boyfriend."

Persephone perked up. "There is? What?"

Dimitra leaned forward, put her elbows on the table and rested her head on her hands. "How do you feel about marriage?"

CHAPTER TWENTY-THREE

Persephone was tense.

"Hey, relax, sis." Zoe pinched her on the arm.

"Ow, bitch!" Persephone complained, holding her arm. They were standing in front of the double doors that housed the mainframe. It was just a glorified computer, but since that computer could think for itself, it could plot the course over generations and had control over life and death over everyone on board, it might as well be their god.

"Now you're focused on me and not on your worry," Zoe said proudly.

Persephone opened her mouth to say something, but there was movement.

The doors slid open.

The sisters gulped.

Persephone hesitated.

Then Zoe shoved her inside with a giggle and the doors shut again.

Persephone slammed on the floor. It was rather unclean, she noticed, having been a floor cleaner for a few months. She pushed herself up and tilted her head up to see the mainframe.

It was more like a light show, blinking lights.

"Colonist," a soft female voice said. It didn't sound synthesized.

"Echo," Persephone grunted. She was upright now, rubbing her palms on her pants. "I have come seeking audience."

"You could have spoken to me through any terminal and comm on the ship," Echo said, her tone not sounding displeased.

"I could, I suppose…" Persephone said, pressing her lower lip. She started to pace up and down and waving frantically as she tried to express herself. "This felt more official, I guess. It's important, what I'm about to ask of you." She suddenly had a paranoid realization and she snorted. "Unless you're intercepting our messages and you already know what I'm about to ask you, making the whole thing pointless."

"I do not intercept personal communications, Persephone. That would violate human rights," Echo said. "That would only happen in case I was worried about the safety of the ship. Even then, I would have forked an instance of myself with that specific task alone, would have investigated, and then she would have reported back to me only if it deemed it relevant. In any case, the instance would have deleted itself, and I would never know the contents."

Persephone stopped and frowned. It was hard to stare down a row of blinking lights. "So… You would have copied yourself, opened my messages, figured out if it was harmful, made a report back to your original self and then made yourself forget about it?"

"Pretty much," Echo said.

"Neat."

"Thanks. But I think you're stalling. No offence."

Persephone's eyes shot up at that remark. "None taken, Echo." She clapped her hands once. "Okay, here's the deal. You know about my relationship, right?"

"The fuzzy bits, yes."

Persephone couldn't help but smirk at that. Echo was funny

sometimes. "Okay. I have a dilemma. On the one hand, I want to be with Trip, make a family, raise babies. Not yet, mind you, but I do want that. It is obviously impossible, I know that. I'm not delusional. And on the other hand, I have a duty on the ship for the next generation. I, unfortunately, have been cursed with the brainpower to understand how important the colony is."

"Indeed, you are," Echo said, and she sounded sad.

"I'm not ready to get pregnant," she chuckled. "Definitely not. But you seem to think that I am, so fine. What do I know? I'm just a stupid human with a squishy brain and limited information. I trust you, Echo. But I wanted to ask if we might bend the rules a little?" She winced as she said the last bit, looking up expectantly.

"What do you have in mind?"

"I'll be impregnated with a diverse seed from the sperm bank, right? I know it's not the same thing, but could we perhaps find a close genetic match to Triptolemus?"

"Ah…" Echo said, with an expression that was thoroughly human. "You believe that that way you can better care for your child. If that's what you want, yes, it's possible. The sperm bank available is extensive. We might even find a familial match. But I wouldn't suggest genofixing an actual copy of your lover's genetic code, that might have unintended consequences for future generations."

Persephone shook her palm at Echo and pressed her lips in an 'o.' "No, no, it's fine. I get it. I just want my kid to look like him, you know? Like if we actually had a child together. His hair, his eyes, his smile."

"That's not how children are-"

Persephone interrupted her. "I know! It's a mix of genes. I'm sure you can simulate an approximation."

"I can, yes," Echo said simply.

"Good," Persephone said, breathing hard. "Thank you, Echo." She turned to leave, then stopped. She added, "For everything you do for us."

"You're welcome."

She walked out to meet Zoe's expectant eyes. "Well? Did she go for it? Did she?"

"Yes…" Persephone groaned and hugged her sister.

She hugged her back. "Then why are you so mopey about it? You did it! Yay?" Zoe sounded confused.

Persephone hugged her tight, then she loosened her embrace and met her eyes. "That was the easy part. Now comes the hard part."

CHAPTER TWENTY-FOUR

"Oh, man, he does not seem to like this," Dimitra whispered to Persephone.

The frown on Trip's face was epic. "You're gonna get worry lines if you stay like that for another five minutes," she said to him.

Trip opened his mouth, blinked slowly, then shut it again. He turned away to look through the window. It wasn't a real window, rather a high-resolution monitor that showed the view from the top floor, like a periscope. The 'window' was illuminating the apartment with a warm reddish glow from the sunset sky, but had no direct line-of-sight with it.

Dimitra tapped her foot and waited, feeling anxious. She looked around the place. "I like your apartment, it's nice." It was a small box downtown, and the rent was astronomic.

Trip turned to her, and said, "Thanks," still frowning.

"Can I get you some water? Let me get you some water," Dimitra said and found the kitchen on her own, rummaged around the cupboards for a glass and brought him some water.

He accepted it with a 'thanks' and drank slowly.

Dimitra decided to let him have his time to process it. She distracted herself by taking in the apartment. It was nice, modern. Clean, which was important, but she could tell it was a bachelor living there. Her gaze fell on the bed. It was unmade, a single bed with dark red sheets, a speaker tape next to it, and a small reading LED light. Dimitra found herself smiling. She did think about having sex with Trip. Every time she imagined it the surroundings were either hazy, or taken from her previous experiences. Now they would be grounded in dark red sheets. She sat on it and ran her fingers along them, grabbing a handful. Just like she would when she would reach her climax underneath him.

"It wont' be mine," Trip said, and Dimitra snapped her attention back to him. It wasn't a question, more like a realisation.

"I'm sorry?" Dimitra asked.

"The kid. It won't be mine."

"No," Dimitra said and let her mouth open in an 'o.'

"But it will look like me, as if it was my own. And Persephone's, with Mendel's pairings and whatnot." He was still frowning, but he didn't seem that shocked now. He was sitting on the corner of his desk, facing her with his body, but not his eyes. Those were persistently locked on some point on the floor.

Dimitra sighed. "Trip... Look, it's a solution. It's not the one you'd like, no. I agree. But what other choice is there? You cannot physically be together, that's a given. And this is just us abusing technology, giving us some wiggle room."

He raised his face towards her and smiled bitterly. "It was your idea, wasn't it?"

Dimitra's instinct was to deny that. She was worried that it would break some of the trust they had managed to build, and that trust was fragile. This whole deal wouldn't work without it. But trust is built when things are out in the open. When you're telling the truth, and expect the other person to do the same. She sighed, raised her chin. "Yes, it was." She pressed her lips.

"Fucking bitch!" Trip snarled and slammed his fist on the desk.

Dimitra flinched, and her eyes darted towards the exit, making sure she had a clear line. Yes, she trusted the man, but how long had she known him really?

With him turning his back on her and his chest heaving, and her sitting on the bed but ready to dash out of there, the air was thick with tension.

And then Persephone spoke. "I know you, Trip. Don't you dare blame Dimitra for this. Yes, she came up with the idea. Which is brilliant, as a matter of fact, and if you can't see that, fuck you. My friend is awesome like that. And she didn't force it on me, it was my choice. I went to see Echo. She agreed to do it. All we need is for you to do a standard DNA test and send the file up to me. She'll take care of the rest."

Trip turned to meet Dimitra's eyes. His were watery, and hers were sad. There was silence.

"Oh, and by the way, if you don't agree to this, I'm gonna go find the first sperm popsicle they have available and shove it up my pussy, then I'm gonna block you forever and live my life alone. Me, my sister and the baby."

Trip shook his head and smiled wide. He was still angry, that much was obvious, but the fact that Persephone knew what to say and how to work him made him have a laugh about it. "Sperm popsicle," he snorted.

"Sperm popsicle," Dimitra snorted back in agreement. "She really is something else, that woman." She stood up and stepped close to Trip, then held his hand inside hers.

Trip looked down at her, his gaze forceful. "I'm sorry, it's-"

"It's okay," Dimitra whispered and ran her fingers along his neckline.

He let his head hang, and she moved in closer, hugging him tight.

Trip sobbed with a sudden shudder that moved her entire body.

Dimitra shushed him softly, kissed him on the ear and pulled his head on her breasts.

"This is too much!" his cry came muffled.

"Shh... It's alright. Let it out," Dimitra said softly, caressing his head on her chest.

Trip cried out loud, and Dimitra held him close.

CHAPTER TWENTY-FIVE

"Wow, sis, you really suck at this job," Zoe said, leaning on the wall.

Persephone was in the middle of doing her new job, but it wasn't going well for her. "It's these damn gloves!"

"How hard can it be to put the right finger in the proper place inside a glove," Zoe scoffed.

Persephone showed her teeth at her, while she was still trying to put the damn things on. "They're sticky, dammit!"

"Perhaps you have clammy hands," Zoe offered unhelpfully.

"Let's see you do it better."

"I didn't ask for this job. You did." Zoe turned around to watch at a group of kids her age in the cafeteria. It was a boy with dark skin, an Asian boy and an Asian girl who looked too similar, so they must have been brother and sister, and another girl, a short brunette.

Persephone instantly got it. She was still fussing around with the gloves, when she suddenly decided, "Who needs five fingers anyway?" And she left her index and middle finger in the same hole. She opened the lid and started scooping out Greek yogurt. "Let's see, four-and-a-half kilos…"

Zoe kept on looking at the group.

Persephone scooped some and threw it on the big cup for further serving, and put it on an electronic scale. "Who has gotten your attention, you little menace?"

"Nobody!" Zoe said far too quickly and far too defensively. She looked away, fiddling with her fork.

Persephone snorted. "Yeah, right. Come on, tell me. It's not like I have any friends on board to share it with."

"You have Hara," Zoe said, her palm up towards her sister.

"I barely know her. And we work together, it's not like we tell each other anything. She's the one doing the talking, she never shuts up." Was this four kilos? No?

"Add more," the smart scales said.

Zoe smirked. "Seriously, sis, when you told me you were getting the night shift at the cafeteria, all I could think about was how you would handle Hara's peppiness."

Persephone sighed. "She's intolerable. Don't tell her I said that." She gathered up the yogurt that fell around the place, she had made a mess. "Huh. Perhaps you do need five fingers to do shit."

Zoe cleaned her teeth with her fork. "I won't."

The smart scales spoke again. "Add a bit more."

"You do it, then!" Persephone screamed at the poor machine.

"Yes…" Zoe drolled, "my sister, the paragon of a person who's got her shit together."

"Ah!" Persephone groaned and pulled the glove off. She scooped some more Greek yogurt and taunted the smart scales. "How do you like that?"

"It will suffice," the scales said with a calm voice.

Persephone turned to her sister, eyes wide. "I can't even argue with the damn thing."

"Don't call it a thing, you're lucky it only has a 0.1

intelligence, or it would have filed a complaint against you by now," Zoe said. She reached in over the counter and forked some veggies, then munched on them.

"They can do that?" Persephone asked. She turned back to the smart scale. "Good scales. Good scales. I'll clean you up, I'm sorry." She did just that.

"Thank you," the scales said.

When she was done, she turned to her sister again. "Come on, tell me. Is it the Asian guy?" She put her elbows on the counter and smirked at her.

"No!" Zoe said defensively once again. She had her mouth full, her cheeks puffy. Bits of green stuff flew out of it.

"Ugh," Persephone said and threw a napkin at her. "Just like at home." She slapped the counter top. "Okay, if you don't wanna tell me, I'll just ask them when they come back for their food and drinks." Persephone went to the slicer. She fiddled with it for a while and then put the roll of meat into the proper spot. She pushed the slider it to slice it neatly, but the meat wasn't sitting well. She put her hand on it and slid it again.

The smart slicer complained. "You are in danger of hurting yourself. Please remove your hand and place it only on the designated areas."

"You do it, then!" Persephone shouted at it.

"Okay, fine," Zoe said, her head down. She looked back at the group. "It's the Asian one."

"I knew it!"

"No…" Zoe breathed out with a sigh. Her chest deflated and her shoulders sagged. "The other Asian one."

Persephone froze and blinked at her. "Oh…" she said softly, her mouth staying in an 'o.' She turned around and bit her lips, checking her out. "She looks cute."

"She is," Zoe giggled and pushed a strand of hair behind her ear.

"I bet she's smart, right?"

"Nope, dump as a cow."

Persephone opened her eyes wide. "Okay…" she finally added after a long silence. She turned back to the smart slicer. "Where do I put my hands on you?" she asked it.

The smart slicer turned on some green LEDs and indicated the designated areas.

"Oh. If only everyone was that easy," Persephone said, and sliced some meat for the day's menu.

CHAPTER TWENTY-SIX

Dimitra was having a great day. She had done her house chores, her meal was spot on, and she'd even done some serious work on her thesis.

So, naturally, it was time for everything to go to shit.

She was humming along, doing her laundry, when the washing machine decided to freeze. 'Updating...' the screen said, and it stopped doing anything.

She slapped the damn thing. "Nonono! Come on, I need this done by tonight," she whined, shoving the pile of laundry to the door. It resisted being opened, but she pulled it out. It made a whirring, screeching sound which she was sure she'd regret later on. Then she shoved the laundry inside the drum and pushed it shut with a groan.

"Right. Okay, sure, do your update or whatever," she said,

blowing a strand of hair off her face.

Nothing changed for five minutes. Then ten. Then fifteen. She kicked the damn thing, "Come on!"

It didn't seem like the situation was gonna change.

"How are we feeling?" Persephone asked in a voice message. Her tone had that innuendo droll. "All ready for tonight?"

"No," Dimitra snapped at her, leaning back on the toilet. "I don't have clean underwear, the dress you picked out for me is in the laundry pile and the damn washing machine decided to brick itself for an automated update."

Her friend wasn't gonna reply for at least forteen minutes, so she went around to see how she could salvage this. She went through her clothes, and it really wasn't looking good. She started streaming and kept sending audio messages, basically thinking out loud. "I don't have any of the clothes we shopped together, so, there's your fantasy gone, right there." She felt tears flooding her eyes. "Dammit!" she sniffled. "I wanted this to be perfect for you, I should have done this yesterday, but I was out all day and then I was tired... Dammit."

She rubbed her face and avoided looking at herself in the mirror. "One disaster at a time." She went in her closet and pulled everything that was serviceable out on the bed. She made sure she looked once over all the articles of clothing, so that Persephone would have time to pick something else. An old skirt, gray and ugly but it went with everything, a yellow sundress, and jeans. It wasn't the best selection. "Got it? Save me, mylady," she said theatrically, then hurried back inside the bathroom. There, she did some things that she really should have done the night before, thus giving time to her skin to settle down and recover, but what the heck? She was late.

"I'm thinking the jeans? It's a classic, after all."

"Yeah, but one time I put them on on a date, they refused to get off me when I wanted to get naked, and the guy had to pull my pants sleeve that had like, suction powers on my thigh, and I pulled away and my leg suddenly kicked uncontrollably and I got him on the nose and we spent the evening in the ER trying to stop the bleeding."

Dimitra winced, sucking in air. "It wasn't pretty."

She threw her things in her bag and then turned towards the bathroom mirror, eyes shut. "I guess I'll have to face it, eventually." She opened her eyes. She looked like a crazy lady with her hair all over the place. She looked tired, she had a zit, and she was feeling less than bangable. "Fuck!" she said out loud, and started to put makeup on.

"Calm down," Persephone said. "Our date will be fine. I know Trip, he doesn't need much. Sure, I wanted it to be perfect, but it really is perfect already," she said, and

Dimitra could hear the smile in her voice.

She stopped, stared at herself in the mirror, holding the eyeliner to the side. "You really mean that? I'm glad." She breathed in deep, then let go, and finally went back to dolling herself up for the big date.

"I think the sundress is the best choice. It looks pretty no matter what, it's like a multi-tool dress. Need to look casual? Sundress. Need to look formal? Sundress. And we can go without panties. That should get us in the mood." Persephone said asynchronously. She had sent another message without having listened to Dimitra's last reply. It was like texting, but weirder. Dimitra had gotten used to it by now, and she liked having Persephone around, even as just a long-distance friend.

She giggled thinking about that. "Hah! I guess me and you are now in an increasing-distance relationship as well. Funny that." She finished her eyeliner, spending the time and making extra sure not to get that stupid crap inside her eye again 'cause it made a mess and stung like a motherfucker, and checked herself out in the mirror.

She did a birdbath once again, it was hot and she had gotten sweaty again from running around like a headless chicken. Some deodorant, some more deodorant, "Let's not risk it. Fuck, I'll carry it in my purse," she said and did exactly that, and then she put on the sundress.

"Yeah..." she smiled, giving it a whirl.

"I'm ready to go on a date," Persephone cheered.

"I feel bangable now." And it sure was breezy.

CHAPTER TWENTY-SEVEN

Triptolemus smiled at the woman across the table and was surprised at how quickly he had adapted to this craziness. Sure, it wasn't ideal, and it felt slightly psychotic speaking to a woman that was double, but they quickly got into a groove. Persephone would say something to their shared channel, so he would hear her voice. And then Dimitra would pick up the slack during the lag and carry on the conversation. Hers was a completely different voice, higher pitched. But they would easily switch gears and Dimitra's reactions seemed exactly like Persephone's. Trip was sure that the girls had practiced a couple of things, or at the very least had talked about a few situations.

For example, he was stunned during their first date, when Dimitra kissed him so casually. Then again, that's exactly what Persephone would have done if she was there in person. That one was definitely arranged in advance.

Their role-play was easy to get into. Dimitra was likeable. Sure, she was shorter and curvier than Persephone, and that broke the illusion many times. However, Trip had to agree with Dimitra that it mattered more whether the surrogate had chemistry with the couple, rather than her being an exact match or whatever. In fact, they had talked about making a proposal to the oversight agency when Dimitra was done with the thesis and gotten some peer reviews to her analysis. But that was for another day.

Now, he had more important things to think about.

"Like my dress?" Persephone squealed naughtily and bit her lip. She scooted over closer to him, dragging the chair on the ground. She lifted the one end and left her thigh exposed to the light of the sunsets.

"Yeah, I love it," he replied, letting his gaze wander around her flesh. Her inner thighs were milky and looked soft. He'd bet they tasted soft too, if he dove in with his face and ran his lips all over them.

Persephone waited for him to enjoy her lovely sight, and then sighed audibly. She raised a delicate finger to his face, followed it, and then lowered it at a spot on her inner thigh. "I'd like a nibble, right there, please." She was looking away at the sunsets.

Trip snorted. "What, now?"

She turned to him, playfully irritated. "Yes, now." She made a pout with her lips that drove him nuts.

Trip looked around, the café wasn't exactly packed, but there were plenty of people around. Of course, this was a lovers' spot, and he could see a lot of wandering hands and embraced couples, that were definitely doing things that they shouldn't be out in public. He turned back to Dimitra, or rather, his girlfriend Persephone, who was still pouting. "What the hell…" he said and leaned down between her legs. At the last second, he decided to get back at her and instead of a playful nibble, he gave her a strong bite. Her flesh was soft and smelled lovely.

"Ouch!" Persephone jerked up.

Trip grinned at her. "I couldn't help myself, love."

She touched his chin. "That's what I like about you, Trip." Then she leaned close and kissed him sloppily, biting his lips.

Persephone's voice came to his ears, which was an impossible feat since she was currently sticking her tongue as far down as it could go inside his mouth. Oh, right, it was actually Dimitra. "Touch my thigh, baby," Persephone said huskily. Her voice was deep, breathy. She was definitely alone in her bunk and was enjoying herself, looking through Dimitra's cybereyes.

Trip had some reservations up until that point. Sure, they had talked about it, and sure, it was nothing more than roleplay. It was one thing talking about having physical sex with another woman, and heck, even the kissing and cuddling was no big deal if you really thought about it. But now he could hear his girlfriend a million kilometres away breathing hard and rubbing her clit while experiencing a hot date with him. So, his reservations promptly evaporated.

She was into this. She wouldn't regret it, it didn't seem like it.

Trip finally let himself give in to the illusion. He grabbed Persephone's back and pulled her closer to him, kissed her back and made her moan, and ran his fingers between her thighs. He explored around for a bit, and was shocked to find that there was nothing stopping him from her pussy. No fabric whatsoever.

He smiled. "You naughty thing."

Persephone took an innocent expression. "I have no idea what you're talking about."

He kissed her again, and pushed his thumb inside her pussy. It was scalding hot. "I feel like a teenager," Trip said when he stopped to come up for air.

"Me too…" Persephone breathed out, her eyes heavy. "I want you, baby," she said, her voice nasal and low, barely a grunt.

"Wanna go back to my place?" Trip asked. To his surprise, he was very anxious about her response. Which was silly, after all. This was his girlfriend, they'd been together for years. Of course, she'd want to come back to his place.

Right?

Persephone pushed his hand away from her privates and stood up, holding her purse. "I thought you'd never ask."

CHAPTER TWENTY-EIGHT

Persephone was about to have sex with her boyfriend for the very first time.

Not literally, but this was the next best thing. Cybersex was good, but it was way over the top by necessity. Like porn, it demanded an unrealistic, excessive performance of the participants. They had no sense of touch so they had to act, to moan, to say dirty things. Even their brief attempt at teledildonics was a failure. Trip had everything available to him, being back on Earth, but Persephone could only print what she was allowed, and a glorified sex toy was not high on her list of priorities when she was lacking basic things like a hair dryer. Not to mention that when they did actually get around to obtaining a functioning pair each, they realised that it did little to bridge the gap between them, those gaping seven light-minutes of empty space. Ever there, ever-increasing at a mind boggling speed. She recycled the teledildo the very next day.

Right now, Trip simply had his top off and stood right in front of her, and Persephone was about to burst already. She ran her fingers down his arm, feeling the skin and the tight muscle. She couldn’t actually feel it, Dimitra did the feeling for her, but Persephone was so close to him she thought she could actually reach out and touch him. She raised her own hand and did just that, keeping her mind in a haze, like unfocusing your eyes to manage to see a magic picture.

"I've been waiting for this," Trip grunted, his chin touching her forehead. That wasn't actually possible, since Persephone wasn't that short but she was willing to give in to this inaccuracy. In a way, it made it even better. Like he was much bigger than her, holding her, digging his nose in her hair and taking a whiff that enchanted him.

His hand touched her elbow, and she felt it, shivering. He ran the back of his fingers along her arm, and her breath caught. She was panting hard, feeling her chest go up and down. She couldn't decide what was best, to open wide and watch the live stream or to shut her eyes and let her imagination run wild, triggered from the images before her.

She decided she had enough of imagination. The real Trip, her real boyfriend, was there.

She hurried and pulled down his pants.

"I… I can't wait anymore," Dimitra said, her voice breaking.

"Want me to stop?" Trip asked, lifting his head between her legs.

"No! But I do want to do it. I'm gonna burst. This is me talking, Dimitra." She winced. "Sorry for breaking the illusion, but you've been down there for thirty minutes."

Trip chuckled and pushed himself upward. His mouth and chin was glistening from her juices. He positioned himself over her, feeling his way around her body with tender gropes and gentle rubs. "This lag sucks. But it was nice getting feedback directly from Persephone."

"I know. But I'm sore!" Dimitra chuckled with a whine.

He leaned down and kissed her on the lips. "It's okay. Any more and I won't be able to move my tongue tomorrow." He pushed his body on top of hers and simply stayed there, feeling his way around.

Dimitra groaned. She wrapped her legs around his waist and almost pulled him right inside her.

"Hey!" Trip complained, but didn't resist. He stopped though, right before entering her. "Let me get my condoms," he grunted, stretching over her towards the nightstand.

"Oh, wait. Trip wait. We need to use plain ones." Dimitra

unwrapped herself with an effort of will and stood up. She grabbed the box of plain condoms she bought, unflavoured and with no spermicide.

She bit the edge and fumbled with it, hopping in place impatiently. Trip was leaning on his side, watching her. She tried to make this a part of the sex, by showing off her expertise and winking at him naughtily.

Of course, she failed, and she fumbled some more with the damn package.

Trip offered a hand. "Want me to-"

"Nope. Got it, here." She took the condom off and prepared it in his hands, pinching the tip and unfolding it a tiny bit. It wasn't like the usual brands, thin or flavoured or any other silliness people bought. It was thick and plain, looking like rubber.

She hopped on the bed and Trip turned on his back, offering his erection.

She put it on, pulled it down and made sure it was tucked firmly in place. She was, after all, going to do a crash test of it. She grabbed his erection and held it left and right, inspecting her work.

Trip snorted. "Good?"

"We're good," Dimitra smiled. "Let's get your girlfriend pregnant."

Persephone wanted to synchronise their orgasms, but that was obviously impossible. Besides, she had already brought herself to the end twice already, and despite the soreness she was feeling, she wanted more.

She craved more.

Trip was on top of her, her legs spread and bouncing up and down in the air. He was fucking her, kissing her, whispering sweet nothings into her ear.

All she could do was to grab the back of his head and pull him down deeper inside her. She licked his arm and neck, felt the saltiness of his sweat, the warmth of his body, and the force of his cock plunging into her.

Trip stopped thrusting and propped himself up on his arms. Panting, he said, "I'm gonna cum, honey."

"Come inside me," Persephone said and kissed him with lust, swirling her tongue around his.

Trip pushed a couple more times as they kissed, grunted, and with a tremor filled her up. He had to break the kiss for breath. After a while, he fell beside her and held her tight in his arms.

Persephone smiled, touching his cheek and looking deep into his wonderful, loving eyes.

Then Dimitra pulled off the condom carefully, pinching the top shut. She stood up and put it in the collection cup. She hopped back to bed, biting her lip, and went in for another snuggle.

CHAPTER TWENTY-NINE

One year later.

"Hey, girl! How did the big day go?" Persephone asked in her voice message.

Dimitra started. She had gotten unused to hearing her voice all the time. Somehow, in-between work and academia and other mundane chores, they'd simply stopped chatting all day. Nothing actually happened to separate the two, it was just that Persephone was crazy busy with the baby and then one day Dimitra didn't want to bother her with her daily inanities and one day became two and two became a week and they hadn't caught up for six months now.

Dimitra turned to her selfie drone and sniffled. It was a newer addition to her arsenal, bought by the university. It was one of a pair, two identical drones that alternated between recording and recharging, keeping you streaming

24/7. Tears welled up in her eyes. "Persephone, I had no idea how much I missed you until I heard your voice!" She rubbed her snot from the tip of her nose, trying to be elegant in front of an audience. "What's up? How's Jason? Send me some recent pics, you neglected that," she added with a pout.

She sent the message and waited. The lag had increased, it took about seven minutes and twenty seconds now. And twice that to get an immediate reply. Which meant she had just enough time to run home and get out of these heels, they were killing her.

She kept on broadcasting asynchronously. Persephone would see these messages at some point and maybe respond at a later time. "Ouch. Heels, what a torture. Trust me, you're lucky you don't wear heels on the ship. Gotta look good for the committee, you know?" She chuckled, and hopped in place, taking one shoe off.

"I can imagine. How did that go?"

"Trip really came through for me. Remember that earlier meeting he arranged for me with the executives? Well, it went terribly. But, somehow a report went up the ladder, some algorithm kicked up the relevant keyword for a decision-maker at the right moment and they called me back a week later!" Dimitra smiled wide, keeping her mouth open in an incredulous expression. "I know, right?"

The lag was noticeable now. She received the baby pics, and went 'Owww!' like any girl does when faced with puffy baby cheeks. She made sure to activate a filter that blurred the baby images for the live stream. "He's so much bigger now! Give him a big kiss from me, will you? Muah, muah," she smacked, sending kisses on the recording.

"What are you doing these days? I know what I'm doing, I'm barely getting enough sleep with this little bastard." Persephone lifted the baby up on the video and snarled at him, showing her teeth in mock anger. Then she kissed his head a million times in a barrage of tiny little pecks. "We're full of energy, aren't we, Jason? We are, we are…," she cooed, fixing his little coat. Then she sing-songed, shaking the baby gently. "What is Dimitra doing, huh?"

"Yeah, I'm always busy with this whole 'Softening the Blow of IDR.'"

Persephone switched back to voice only. "Things got nasty, Jason needed a change of diapers. Um, sorry, IDR?"

"Oh, right. It's like LDR, but different." Dimitra called a self-driving taxi and went to the only place that felt right for her.

"Snort. Okay, I'll bite, what's LDR?"

"Long Distance Relationship."

"Right. So the equivalent is Increasing Distance Relationship, got it."

"I asked around, and found a scientific explanation for the effect we experienced, the Body

Transfer Illusion. Search for 'rubber hand illusion,' there are a ton of videos online. It's like an experiment where they place a rubber hand on the table, then trick your senses to think it's your own. When touched or pinched, the brain thinks it actually does feel what a normal hand would feel in its place. In our case, I was the rubber hand, and you were feeling the connection. Anyway, today they decided to move things forward. The paper, the research, the funding. It's all happening, finallywa!"

She paused, waiting seven minutes and twenty seconds for it to get there, biting her lip all the way. She looked silly, but it meant a lot to her. The response would take the same amount of time to get back, but she wanted to get the timing right.

She looked around at the cafe. The smell was exactly the same, that of aromatic drinks and fresh air. The sky was beautiful, and the sun was setting as usual. Right next to it, the afterburner sunset shone dimly. She knew that it had gotten dimmer than last year, but it wasn't noticeable to the naked eye. She sniffed, looked around, and turned off her selfie drone. Instead of grabbing a chair, she leaned against the railing, wanting to reach against the sky, to be as close to the generation ship as possible, even if it was just a couple of meters.

She checked the clock. Then she recorded for Persephone alone, with tears in her eyes, "I couldn't have done it without you. Thank you, so much."

At the same moment, the asynchronous response from Persephone arrived. "I wanted to thank you, Dimitra. I wouldn't have this bundle of joy if it weren't for you."

Dimitra spoke over her friend and took a second to realise what had happened, that immediate connection across seven minutes and twenty light-seconds of space. Then she burst into laughter, happier than she had ever been.

The End

Leave a review on the store you got this from or on Goodreads.

For more stories like these, join the Mythographers and get your free starting library in your email:

https://mythographystudios.com/join

www.ingramcontent.com/pod-product-compliance
Lightning Source LLC
LaVergne TN
LVHW041149150826
845673LV00001B/109

* 9 7 9 8 6 6 7 9 1 1 6 7 8 *